# Out on a Limb

# Out on a Limb

Gail Banning

KEY PORTER BOOKS

**Library and Archives Canada Cataloguing in Publication**

Banning, Gail
Out on a limb / Gail Banning.

ISBN 978-1-55470-012-7

I. Title.

PS8603.A627O98 2008 jC813'.6 C2007-905542-7

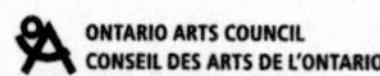


The publisher gratefully acknowledges the support of the Canada Council for the Arts and the Ontario Arts Council for its publishing program. We acknowledge the support of the Government of Ontario through the Ontario Media Development Corporation's Ontario Book Initiative.

We acknowledge the financial support of the Government of Canada through the Book Publishing Industry Development Program (BPIDP) for our publishing activities.

Key Porter Books Limited
Six Adelaide Street East, Tenth Floor
Toronto, Ontario
Canada M5C 1H6

www.keyporter.com

Text design: Marijke Friesen
Electronic formatting: Alison Carr

Printed and bound in Canada

08 09 10 11 12 5 4 3 2 1

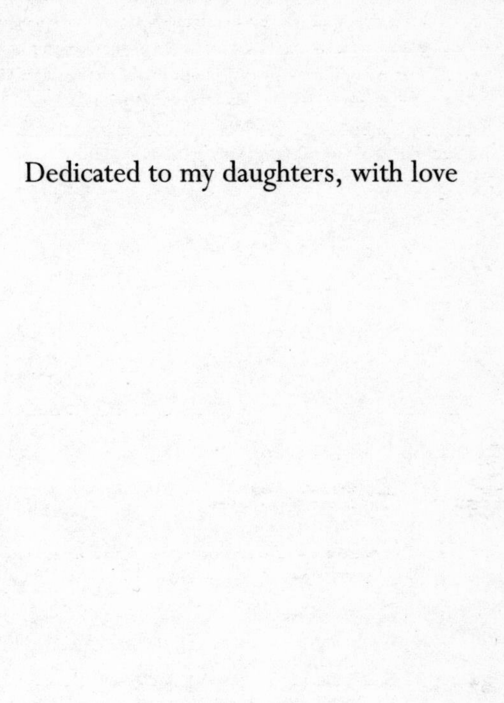

Dedicated to my daughters, with love

## June 30

*They're here again. The total strangers who are my family. And this time they plan to stay.*

*I look down on them from my turret. They are beyond my meadow, on the far side of my stream, at the edge of my woods. Distance makes them tiny. I wave my sterling-silver bell, but Mr. Bickert doesn't hear it, or he pretends not to. My sterling-silver bell belongs to another century. I remember this and reach for my cell phone instead. I speed-dial number one. "Mr. Bickert," I say, "my binoculars please. And quickly." He is quick, for once. He thumps up the turret stairs with them before the strange family has reached my stream.*

*"Your binoculars, Madam," he says, placing them in my waiting hand. The binoculars, like so many of my things, are embossed with my full name, Lydia Florence Augustine McGrady. Except for Mr. Bickert, there is no one at all in the Manor to read my embossing and my engraving. All that it does is remind me of who I am.*

*I raise my binoculars and get the little family in my scope. Refocusing, I close the distance between us. I can see the four of them better now. The man with that little scruff of a goatee that seems to be all the fashion these days, for heaven only knows what reason. He must be David, the grandson of my dead brother. And that woman in a man's undershirt with the tattoo around her bicep like a common sailor—that must be his wife, Andrea. But it's at the two girls that I keep directing my aim. The bigger one, with hair shining like sheet copper, her name is Rosamund. The little one is called Matilda. They've been given good old-fashioned names at least, not India or Hunter or Ocean, or whatever other nonsense one sees in the birth announcements these days.*

*They look defenceless, this strange estranged family with all that they own in four wheelbarrows.*

*They've taken it upon themselves to bridge my stream with a boardwalk of planks. Rosamund's wheelbarrow tips off the plank bridge and she wades down the stream in slow motion after her floating clothes. Afterwards, her family all sits on my meadow. They often look over here at Grand Oak Manor, but they don't see me. I am hidden behind my stained-glass window. I watch them from a transparent pane. They never can tell when they are being watched.*

*After awhile they spring to their feet, laughing. They run, wheelbarrows bumping, toward the giant oak. They are young, and my binoculars don't close the distance of years between us. I put my binoculars down and my estranged family becomes tiny again.*

*I wonder what they will do when they find what is waiting for them.*

| | |
|---|---|
| NOTEBOOK: | #1 |
| NAME: | Rosamund McGrady |
| SUBJECT: | The Infamous Will |

We were nearly homeless when we made our big discovery.

We still had a home then, but we were about to lose it. Developers were going to tear down our apartment building because it was old and shabby. Inside you could peel off paint in big flakes, and outside you could pry bits of coloured glass from the stucco. After it was ripped down they were going to replace it with luxury townhomes called Sandringham Mews, of all weird names. The developer had put up a big sign showing the fountain and miniature canals that would be in front of the luxury townhomes. The canals and fountain looked like a fun change from peeling paint and picking stucco, but we weren't going to be living in Sandringham Mews. Too expensive.

We had to find another place to live, and it had to be somewhere cheap. "Something will turn up," Mom said. She sounded all positive and cheery, but that never means much. She sounds that way pretty well all the time. Personally, I was not optimistic.

We had been apartment hunting for three Saturdays already, and things did not look good.

The first place we'd gone to see was a basement suite that smelled like a combo of boiled cabbage, cat pee and the bottom layer of a laundry hamper. When my sister Tilley and I held our noses, Dad nudged me with his elbow. "That's rude," he whispered, so the only way we could protect ourselves was to try to turn our nostrils inside out. The living room of this place had tiny windows way over my head, so high up that you couldn't see anything out of them except the underside of dandelions. Still, they were better than the bedroom window, which was totally covered on the outside by a pile of dirt. That bedroom was like a furnished grave.

"Yuck!" Tilley and I declared, as soon as we left the basement suite and were back on the street.

"Yuck is right," Mom and Dad agreed, much to our relief.

The next place was an apartment right at the intersection of two big highways. The apartment *looked* okay, but every time a truck went by the dishes and knick-knacks would hop up and down on the shelves and we all had to stop talking until the traffic roar faded. Also, the air in that place was at least 40 percent motor-vehicle exhaust.

Then there was the place where the glass lobby door had been all smashed and stuck back together with silver duct tape. We buzzed the intercom for the landlord, and he came lurching through the lobby like it was a ship deck in a storm. "Drunk," I informed Tilley. His arm was all bandaged up with the same silver duct tape that was on the door. We didn't even go inside.

On our third house-hunting Saturday I thought we'd found the perfect apartment. The newspaper ad listed an affordable price, and when we got to the building we saw white lace curtains in every window, new blue paint outside and a front garden full of very organized tulips. We were all jiggling each other's arms in happiness when the landlady appeared. "Oh," she said, looking down at Tilley and me as though we were a pair of overflowing garbage cans. "This is a child-free building. I'm *sorry*," she said, which she obviously was not in the slightest. Even Mom looked a bit discouraged as we climbed back into our car. They were going to tear down our apartment on June 30. That was only two weeks away, and we still had no place to go.

We made our discovery that night. Dad had dragged all the cardboard boxes up from our basement storage locker. While Tilley and I tossed popcorn into each other's mouths, Mom and Dad sorted through old income tax returns and appliance warranties, figuring out what to throw away before the move. Some documents went back into file folders. Most went into the recycling. And then Mom found it.

"David, what's this?" she asked my dad. The paper she held had turned golden brown, like a treasure map, and it had big, antique-looking letters. "*Last Will and Testament of Magnus Everard Granville McGrady*," Mom read.

"Who's that?" I asked.

"Your great-great-grandfather," Dad said. "This must be his infamous will. I've never seen it before. I didn't even know we had a copy."

"What's infamous?" Tilley asked.

"Famous for being bad," I told her.

Dad read over Mom's shoulder. "*To Tavish Elliot Granville McGrady, who was once my son, I bequeath the estate treehouse. To my daughter Lydia Florence Augustine McGrady, I bequeath my beloved Grand Oak Manor, and the balance of my estate.*"

"What does *that* mean,"Tilley wanted to know.

"Well, your Great-great-grandfather Magnus, was mad at his son, your Great-grampa Tavish," Dad said. "So Magnus wrote this will saying that when he died, Great-grampa wouldn't get his money or his mansion or anything. Instead of dividing things up between his two kids, Magnus gave it all to his daughter, and he didn't give Great-grampa anything."

"That's not fair,"Tilley said. That's something she says a lot, but this time I agreed.

"But does that will give Great-grampa a treehouse?" I asked.

"Well, yeah," Dad said. "As an insult."

"So what's the story with this treehouse?" Mom asked.

"Don't really know," Dad said. "There was a treehouse on the estate when your Great-grampa was a boy, but I never saw it. Obviously. The split in our family happened a long time before I was even born. Great-grampa used to talk about the treehouse though. It was way up in some humongous tree. A giant northern oak, maybe? Something really rare anyway. He even slept up there sometimes."

"Cool!" Tilley said. "Can we go see it?"

"I doubt if it's still there, all these years later," Dad said, "and even if it is, it would be on private property.

Your Great-grampa's sister, Lydia, still lives on the estate. And she's a total stranger to us, even though she is your great-great-aunt."

My Great-grampa died when I was four years old, when a mudslide swept his van off the highway and into the river.

"Dad," I asked, "who did Great-grampa leave *his* money and property and stuff to, when he died?"

"To Grampa, what there was of it." Grampa had been driving the van and he also died in the same accident, along with my Grandma and aunt. Fortunately, I was too little at the time to fully experience tragedy.

"Well, who did Grampa leave *his* property to?"

"To me," Dad said. "But he didn't have much, you know."

"No, I know Grampa was sort of poor," I said. "But if this Great-great-grandfather Magnus left everything to Great-grampa, and Great-grampa left everything to Grampa, and Grampa left everything to you, wouldn't that make the treehouse *ours*?"

"Technically, I guess," Dad said. "But Rosie, the treehouse part of the will is just a mean joke, you know."

"Please, *please* can we go see the treehouse," Tilley begged.

"Oh Tilley," Dad said. "I'm sure it's fallen apart by now."

"Shouldn't we at least check though?" I asked. "We could go there for a family walk. You and Mom love family walks. We could at least *try* to see it, couldn't we?"

"Try to see it?" Dad said. "Well, I guess so. If you really want to."

"We really want to," I said.

"Really, *really* want to," added Tilley.

"Okay then," said Mom. "That's what we'll do."

| NOTEBOOK: | #2 |
| --- | --- |
| NAME: | Rosamund McGrady |
| SUBJECT: | Giant Oak |

To check out the treehouse, we drove way across town to a fancy neighbourhood. I'd never been there, but Mom and Dad knew the area because it's near the university where they were doctoral students. The university only gives doctorate degrees to people who have studied forever and ever and written an endless nightmare essay called a thesis. Dad was taking entomology, which is the study of bugs. His thesis was about how to get good insects to eat harmful ones so that mankind won't have to use toxic chemical pesticides anymore. Mom was taking linguistics, and for her thesis she was trying to invent a language that could be spoken and understood by both humans and apes.

"I think we'll park here," Dad said, pulling up to the curb. On one side of the street were great big houses. On the other side there was nothing but woods.

"Are we at Great-great-aunt Lydia's?" Tilley asked.

"No," Dad said. "We're at the edge of the University Endowment Lands, but if we walk a mile or two through the woods, we'll get to the back of her estate. We'll sneak in that way, so she doesn't come charging at us with a *No Trespassing* sign."

We slammed our car doors and walked from the sidewalk onto a trail. At first it was like any other trail through the woods, with squashed pop cans under bushes and potato-chip bags in twigs, but as we walked along it got prettier and prettier. After we'd gone a long way, we came to an old stone wall, as high as my head.

"If I'm not mistaken," Dad said, "this wall is the edge of Great-great-aunt Lydia's property." It isn't easy getting over a wall that high. Tilley stood on Dad's clasped hands and got boosted over. I did the same, and jumped to the ground beside Tilley, all thrilled at our sneakiness. Then came Mom. I'm not sure how Dad made it without a boost, but somehow he did.

On the inside of the wall the woods were even nicer. There were emerald green ferns, and ruffly pink rhododendron blossoms, and moss like dark-green velvet. These woods went on and on. "I can't believe that this is *all* Great-great-aunt Lydia's property," I said.

"Yup," sighed Dad. "It's quite the inheritance that Great-grampa missed out on."

We came to a stream with a great big meadow on the far side. The stream wasn't deep, but it was fast, and there was no bridge. We crossed it by leaping from rock to rock. Tilley didn't quite make the last jump, and she soaked a runner and a sock.

"Wow," Tilley said as we stood on the edge of the

meadow looking downstream. "Is *that* Great-great-aunt Lydia's place?"

"That's it," Dad said. "Grand Oak Manor." Way across the meadow was a mansion like a little castle, with turrets and everything. We all stood staring until I suddenly remembered why we were there. I turned around. Way across the meadow, standing all by itself, was the giant oak tree. It was incredibly, unbelievably, impossibly enormous, like it was Photoshopped in, or something. It rose way, way, way up above normal tree height, and spread itself into the sky.

"The treehouse tree!" Tilley shouted. We both ran for it, Tilley's runner spurting little jets of water the whole way. I slowed when the massive tree trunk filled my entire field of vision. Stepping forward, I touched it in amazement. It was as big around as a traffic circle. I tilted my head back and looked up. I couldn't see a single speck of sky, just the green of a billion leaves.

Tilley would climb absolutely anything, even streetlamps, and I could see that she was already figuring out a route up this colossal tree. There were a few ancient-looking boards nailed to the trunk, making a random kind of ladder, and there were also bumps and gnarly places in the bark. It was enough for Tilley. She started to climb.

My parents ran, calling to get down. Tilley pretended not to hear. I tested a foothold on a board and went after her, pretending I didn't hear either. I was way too eager to find the treehouse to wait around on the ground.

I climbed fast. With the boards and the natural footholds, it wasn't hard. Part way up, the trunk divided into big branches. I climbed off at an angle up one of the branches, following what was left of the boards. "Rosie," Dad kept yelling from below. On his seventh or eighth yell I looked down to the bottom of the tree, expecting to see Dad and Mom with freaked-out faces. What I did see was Mom and Dad, far, far, far below me, in miniature. Their faces were dots. I couldn't believe how high I was. Suddenly the tree seemed to tilt and the meadow seemed to rush around.

"Wow," my little sister yelled, her voice way above me. I breathed. If she could do it, I could too. I started climbing again, but really carefully this time. I made sure not to look down any lower than my foothold. I focused on the old boards and the rough bark of that massive branch, and my own knuckles, white from clutching. A billion heartbeats later I saw Tilley's runners, one dusty and one glistening wet, standing on wooden floorboards. I was part way through a trap door. I crawled through and rested my knees on the floorboards, glad to have something solid underneath me.

"Come on Rosie, get up! Let's go see it."

I got to my feet. "It's still here," I said, and then I just stared. The treehouse was better than my very best daydreams. Tilley and I were on a big porch, and there in the middle was a tiny cottage, with real glass windows and an arched door. When I pushed on the brass handle the door stayed shut, but Tilley and I butted it open and shoved inside.

"Wow," I said as my eyes adjusted to the gloom. "No wonder Great-grampa loved this place." There were six walls, with six giant oak branches cutting through the six corners. Three bunks were built in to one of the walls. There was a velvety layer of dirt over everything, but the treehouse smelled really nice, like the inside of a cedar chest.

We could hear Dad getting closer, yelling at us for climbing up without permission. When he stopped mid-sentence we knew that he had seen the treehouse. "Amazing," we heard Mom say a moment later. They both came inside. Mom's fingertips traced and traced the rough bark of the massive oak branches. Dad opened the grimed-over windows, and we all stood looking at the sudden view over Great-great-aunt Lydia's woods. Beyond the oak branches was a sea of treetops in every possible colour of green: blue green, silver green, golden green, creamy green, and lots of plain green green. Birds flitted around singing complicated songs. I was filling up with this fabulous weird feeling. I couldn't remember when I'd felt it before, and then I did. It was from my dreams about flying.

"I know," Tilley said. "Let's live *here*!"

Dad just laughed, the way grown-ups always laugh at their kids' ideas. Then Mom turned from the window, looking sort of dazed.

"I think Tilley's right," she said, turning toward Dad. "I think we *should* live here."

Dad laughed again, but he didn't seem so sure of himself this time. "Andrea," he said. "It's all very nice for a treehouse, but we can hardly live here."

"Why not?" said Mom. "It's ours."

"Only technically," said Dad.

"What's wrong with technically?" asked Mom.

"Andrea, it's a treehouse. There's no electricity," said Dad.

"Mankind lived thousands of years without electricity," said Mom.

"There's no running water," said Dad.

"There's a stream right down there," said Mom. "We're smart people. We could figure something out."

"*Andrea*."

"Don't say 'Andrea' in that condescending voice, as though you've made some sort of valid point," said Mom. "We'd save a pile of money on rent, you know. And we'd be five minutes from the university."

"Come on, Andrea! It's not the slightest bit practical."

"You're making the assumption that we should be practical," said Mom. "Maybe we should be adventurous."

"We've got kids to think of," said Dad.

"Kids like adventure," said Mom.

"We do!" said Tilley, or maybe it was me, or maybe it was both of us. "We love it! We want to live here!"

"Oh, David, look out the window! Listen to the birds! How can you think about writing rent cheques every month for some crappy apartment over a brake-and-muffler shop when this place is *ours*!" Mom was raising her voice. She is a cheerful person, but a lack of enthusiasm can make her really mad.

Dad said nothing. That's the way he argues.

"Consider it at least," said Mom.

"I'll consider it," said Dad.

We had our Sunday picnic sitting on the porch outside the treehouse, gazing through the banisters. Tilley elbowed me and pointed down. A deer stood drinking in the stream below us. When it heard the lemonade pour from our Thermos it looked around all big-eared, and its white rump bounded for the woods. We ate our peanut-butter-and-banana sandwiches. Long after they were finished, we sat waiting for the deer to come back. "I guess we'd better get going," Dad said finally. Cautiously, we all climbed down the oak tree.

I heard my parents considering the treehouse when I was in bed that night. They were murmuring in the living room, on the other side of my bedroom wall. I lay as still as a dead body to hear what they were saying, but it didn't work. Every time I caught a couple of words, a car would squeal its tires; or our fridge would get the shakes; or Tilley would rustle in the other bed; or someone would slam a dumpster lid. I had no idea how the considering was going when I finally fell asleep.

NOTEBOOK: #3

NAME: Rosamund McGrady

SUBJECT: Legal Rights

The results of the considering were announced the next morning.

"Well, it's unanimous," Dad said as he buttered his toast. "We're moving into the treehouse."

"We are?" I crashed my chair backward when I jumped up to hug Dad, but nobody got annoyed. Nobody wanted to spoil the mood.

All I wanted to do was celebrate, and it killed me to have to go off to school. Tilley and I got home in record time that afternoon. We burst into our apartment at 3:34 to find Mom and Dad sitting at the kitchen table with their friend Clarkson, who was a law student. Clarkson had already written a letter to Great-great-aunt Lydia, claiming our rights under the will. Clarkson's letter said that in his legal opinion, we were entitled not just to the treehouse and the oak tree, but also to a certain amount of the surrounding land. We also had a right to pass through

Great-great-aunt Lydia's land to get to and from the treehouse. In addition, Clarkson said, we were entitled to riparian rights, which means rights to the stream. Clarkson's letter said that we would begin making improvements to the treehouse immediately, and we would move in on June 30. Clarkson's letter all by itself didn't seem too friendly, so Mom and Dad wrote a letter to Great-great-aunt Lydia, too. Their letter introduced the four of us, and said that we hoped past family conflicts wouldn't keep us from getting to know each other. We folded Clarkson's letter and Mom and Dad's letter into an envelope. Then, all of us walked to the post office and mailed the letter off by ultra extra-special delivery to Grand Oak Manor, Number 9 Bellemonde Drive.

There were only thirteen days until our apartment building was going to be torn down, and there was lots to do to make the treehouse fit for occupation. We were so busy that Tilley and I got to skip school to help. The very first thing we did was make the climb to the treehouse less dangerous. We made a wooden ladder going all the way up the trunk, along the branch, and through the trap door in the porch. Next, we made a homemade elevator out of pulleys and rope and a big garbage bucket cradled at the end. 'Dumbwaiter' is the word for this kind of device. Tilley begged for a ride up to the treehouse in the dumbwaiter, but Mom and Dad said the dumbwaiter was strictly for inanimate objects.

The dumbwaiter's very first load of inanimate objects was cleaning supplies. We pulled our broom out of the dumbwaiter and swept out all the dried-up spiders and cobwebs. We dug out our Windex and washed away generations of grime until a new golden-green light slanted through the windows. We dug out our furniture oil and polished the wooden walls until they shone like new chestnuts.

Next we worked on plumbing. We designed the system ourselves. It featured an old-fashioned iron pump on the treehouse porch, to pump stream water up through a plastic pipe along the tree trunk. The pipe included filters for straining out parasites and stuff. It was a cool design, but gadgets didn't fit other gadgets the way they were supposed to, and this led to frustration. Tilley and I even heard the occasional swear word. In the end though, we got it working.

For our heating system, we got a wood-burning pot-bellied cast-iron stove. It was free on Ebay, probably because it was so heavy that nobody else wanted it. Moving it to the treehouse was a problem. "It would be so much easier to bring it in by Bellemonde Drive," Mom said. "If we could drive onto the driveway of Grand Oak Manor, we'd just have to worry about getting it out through the Manor garden and across the meadow. That's so much shorter than dragging it all the way through the woods. Do you suppose Great-great-aunt Lydia would mind?"

There was no way of knowing. Great-great-aunt Lydia had not replied to Clarkson's or Mom and Dad's letters, and in all of our trips to the treehouse we'd never caught a single glimpse of her. We'd seen gardeners clipping hedges and watering flowers in the Manor garden, but never Great-great-aunt Lydia. "I don't think we should push our luck," Dad said, so he and some of his friends tied the stove to a trolley and pushed it down the long, bumpy path through the woods. When they got to the stream they untied the stove and rolled it across the stream bottom.

The very hardest part was getting the stove up to treehouse level. We tied it securely into the dumbwaiter and six of Dad's friends cranked the winch until the stove levitated slowly off the ground. Before it was even halfway up to the treehouse their necks were purple and throbbing with veins. I waited in suspense for the stove to plummet to the centre of the earth. It was a big relief to get it safely onto the porch. Dad and his friends put the stove in the centre of the treehouse, and added a sheet-metal chimney that went out the roof and up past the highest branches so that no sparks would ever come into contact with the oak tree. My job was to keep the friends supplied with the cans of beer we had chilling in the stream.

"Now that was hard work," Dad said when the stove was finally in and the friends had gone. He leaned against the banister and turned his beer can upside down into his mouth. "I sure hope Great-great-aunt Lydia isn't about to come brandishing a court order to get us off her property."

"She won't, David," Mom said. "If she really didn't want us moving in, she'd have done something to stop us already. My guess is that she's glad for a chance to reconnect with her family. That's how I'd feel if I was an old lady with a big, empty mansion and no one of my own." We all looked across the meadow to Grand Oak Manor. As usual, there was no sign of Great-great-aunt Lydia.

"Dad," I said. "You know how Great-great-grandfather Magnus was so mad at Great-grampa that he cut him out of his will?"

"Mmhmm," said Dad.

"Well, I don't get how he could be so mad at his very own son."

"Oh, Rosie," Dad said. "Grown-ups think up all kinds of reasons for getting mad at each other."

"But what was *his* reason," I asked.

"I don't know. Great-grampa never said. He tended to keep his past to himself. And he never, ever talked about family. The rift was Great-grampa's big secret."

About the only secret we'd ever had in my family was where the leftover Halloween candy was hidden, so the idea of an old, important secret intrigued me. "But why do you *think*," I asked.

"I don't know, Rosie," Dad said. "This is not one of those things that I know but won't tell you. It's a complete mystery to me."

"Great-grampa Tavish married Isobel pretty young, didn't he?" Mom asked. "Maybe Magnus didn't approve of the marriage."

"Could be," said Dad.

"And then didn't he leave the country for years and years and design theatre costumes in England?" Mom said. "Maybe Magnus thought that was a dumb career choice for the son of a lumber baron."

"Maybe." Dad stood up. "Come on, we've got another full day here tomorrow. We should go back to the apartment and get some rest."

The days leading up to June 30 sped by. We measured the treehouse, and took notes, and made trip after trip to Home Depot. On June 29 we had a yard sale. It was weird to see our toaster and our television and our computer monitor on the grass outside of our apartment building, blinking at the daylight. It was weird to watch strangers walk off with my ice skates and Tilley's Barbie Dream

House. It was necessary, though, to get rid of most of our stuff. There's not much storage space in a treehouse.

The day after the yard sale was demolition day. The foreman of the demolition crew stood in his hard hat in our apartment while Mom knelt on the floor, taping up cardboard boxes. "So how are we doing here," he asked, his voice bouncing around our emptied-out living room.

"Good. We're out of here." Mom straightened and held a cardboard box out to him. He looked a bit surprised, but he unfolded his arms and took it. I looked around our apartment one last time, but there wasn't much to see. Nothing was left but the wire coat hangers pinging in the closet. I picked up my cardboard box and followed my family. We all stepped over the yellow tape that surrounded our apartment building. *DANGER! DO NOT ENTER!* it said.

"Thanks for your patience," Dad said to the foreman.

"No problem," the foreman said, taking his cardboard box out to our car. We all loaded our boxes into the trunk. The demolition crew sent a German shepherd through our apartment building to make sure there was no one still in there, unconscious in a bathroom or something. Then they sounded a big horn that was enough to make anyone jump out of his skin, unconscious or not.

We watched the demolition from across the street, which was as close as the crew would let us get. The wrecking truck lumbered closer to our building, manoeuvred its boom into position and swung its wrecking ball. There was a surprisingly delicate sound of shattering glass. Our living room and bedroom windows were gone, and other windows too. The wrecking ball swung again, and this time the sound was more the sort of major crashing you would expect. The stucco, whose glass bits we had picked out so patiently, fell away in big slabs. The wrecking ball swung again and again. Our side of the apartment building wobbled, then hesitated, then collapsed into billowing dust. The home I'd lived in all my life was gone.

We drove toward the woods and parked. We transferred everything from our car trunk into four rented wheelbarrows. Pushing all our worldly possessions before us, we set off on the path to our new home.

NOTEBOOK: #4

NAME: Rosamund McGrady

SUBJECT: Ripped to Shreds

It was a long way to push a wheelbarrow. Roots the size of boa constrictors got in the way. Then there was the plywood ramp we had built to get over the stone wall that surrounded Great-great-aunt Lydia's woods. I pushed my wheelbarrow up the ramp with all my might, but the force of gravity pushed right back. I couldn't imagine how hard it must have been getting our stove over it. Then there was the stream. We'd bridged it with planks but I got my wheelbarrow too close to the edge. It flipped itself into the stream and took me along with it. Water flowed up my nostrils. I blinked to see Tilley's pink pyjama top swimming in the current. "After them," Mom pointed, and I waded downstream, slipping over river rocks. I snagged the pyjama top and flung it in an arc of droplets to the meadow. Then I went after her pyjama bottoms, her hoodie and her undies. "My triceratops sweatshirt!" Tilley yelled, hopping as though it were a drowning child. "It's getting away!" It looked as though the sweatshirt would slide away in the rapids, but a tangle of twigs snagged it. When I sloshed up to the sweatshirt I saw something else clinging to the criss-crossed twigs. It was a long, ragged strip of blue paper, covered with handwriting. The ink had blurred, but the torn-up words were still readable.

e McGrady
t confess it w
d forgotten th
afraid th
hope you w
ives. It turns
possessed a
tree house i
It turns o
you are who
it turns ou
e forgive m
welcome I'
e old bones
h ground. I
ation fo
someday soon

The writing was shaky, but fancy too, as though the writer had taken special handwriting lessons.

"Come on, Rosie," Dad called. "Let's get going."

"Just a second," I called back. "I've found something weird. I think it's a letter. Part of one."

"A letter? What would a letter be doing in there?" Dad asked.

I waded upstream, the current tugging at my ankles. "I think Great-great-aunt Lydia wrote it," I said, carefully handing the torn blue strip to Mom.

"I doubt it," Dad said. "The Manor is downstream from here. More likely somebody upstream wrote it."

"I don't think so," I said. "It says our name. And it mentions the treehouse."

Mom smoothed the torn strip. "It says welcome," she read, showing it to Dad. "It's a letter of welcome."

"A letter of welcome, ripped to shreds," Dad said.

"How come she ripped it?" Tilley wanted to know.

"I wonder," said Mom. "Maybe this is a practice copy?"

Dad looked doubtful. "And instead of putting the practice copy in the garbage or recycling, she threw it in the stream?"

"That's bad for the environment," Tilley said.

"Maybe the scrap is a puzzle she wants us to figure out," I said.

"But how could she possibly know we'd find it?" Dad objected. "If the clothes hadn't fallen in the stream, we never would have."

We all looked at each other, waiting for improved theories. Our brains were whirring away, but coming up with nothing. "Well," said Dad, "let's get the rest of this stuff across the bridge." I threw Tilley's drowned sweatshirt to the meadow and took the torn blue strip back from Mom. Folding it carefully into my wallet, I waded off to look for the rest of the letter.

"I can't find any more pieces," I reported to my family.

They were sitting with the wheelbarrows at the meadow's edge, dangling their feet in the stream and passing a water bottle. I sat beside them and squirted water down my throat. We all kept looking up at the mansion, hoping for our very first glimpse of Great-great-aunt Lydia. But there was no movement.

"Okay," Dad said. "Let's be on our way. Last one to the giant oak is a rotten egg!"

"'Rotten egg' is such a lame insult," I said, but I grabbed my wheelbarrow anyway and ran across the meadow. I reached the giant oak before anyone else, so I saw it first.

"What's this?" Mom said as she came barrowing up behind me. At the base of the oak tree was a big pink and yellow flower arrangement. It would have been amazing, except that it had been destroyed. It was smashed sideways on the hard ground between the oak roots. I knelt down and turned it right side up. The stems were all bent, as though every single flower had had its neck snapped.

"They must be from Great-great-aunt Lydia," said Mom. "She must have brought them as a housewarming present. They must have fallen off the root where she left them."

"Maybe," said Dad.

"Well, what else," asked Mom.

Dad shrugged. "They sure had one hard landing."

"Well, flowers are delicate," Mom said. "They can't have been here long, that's for sure. They aren't even withered. We can probably save some."

I helped Mom pull the broken stems out of the florist foam. I pulled out a clear plastic stick with a clip at the end. "There's one of these things that you stick a note into," I said. "But no note."

"Because it's been ripped up and thrown into the stream," said Dad.

"Maybe a raccoon ripped it," said Tilley. "'Cause I've seen raccoons at the stream, and they have real hands just almost like people."

"Yeah, maybe Tilley," said Dad. We all nodded, unconvinced. Once again we stood around, waiting for a good theory to materialize out of the summer air.

"Who knows," Dad said finally.

"Can't say I get it either," said Mom. "Let's unpack."

I put a cardboard box of dishes in the dumbwaiter, climbed up to the porch and winched them up. I brought my box inside the arched doorway, into the kitchen we had made. We'd put up a whole bunch of shelves above and below the windows. In one of the six corners, we'd made a tiled counter around the giant oak branch. On the counter was a big water container with a spigot. It was going to be our kitchen tap. Right next to it was the plastic washbasin that was going to be our kitchen sink.

I opened the flaps of my box and unwound the newspaper bundles inside. I hung our mugs on our hooks, and put our plates on our shelves. Mom cut the stems of the broken-necked flowers and arranged them in a bowl on the table that folded out from the wall. I stood back to admire it all.

"Smell those lilies," Mom said. "They're so sweet."

"Really sweet," I said, breathing in.

"They make me feel sick," Tilley said, covering her nose. It was true. The scent seemed to have gone from heavenly to poisonous in a few breaths.

"They are a bit much for such a small space," Dad said, and we moved them to the great outdoors on the porch.

Back inside, we kept unpacking. We worked until the sunset coated everything in the treehouse with transparent colour, like apricot skin. "You kids must be famished," Mom said, and she got a container of cold Kentucky Fried Chicken from the tiny propane fridge under the counter. Dad took out a bottle of champagne and brought it to the arched doorway. The cork flurried though oak leaves. He poured champagne for himself and Mom into Plexiglas goblets, and sparkling apple juice for Tilley and me. "A toast," Dad said, raising his glass. "To adventure." The four of us clinked glasses, or tried anyway. Plexiglas doesn't clink all that well.

Long after the chicken was gone, we sat around on the treehouse porch, swatting mosquitoes and sipping our celebration beverages. The deer was back at the stream. Way across the meadow, lights were coming on in the turrets of Grand Oak Manor. So Great-great-aunt Lydia was there, I thought, even if we'd never seen her. We stared at the golden rectangles of light, hoping for other signs of life. There were none.

"Well, I for one am exhausted," Mom said after a long silence. "Therefore, it is your bedtime."

"Bedtime! Since when do I have a bedtime?"

"Since now that we all share a room," Mom said, rummaging in a box on the porch. "Here. From the camping store. Our lighting system." She handed me a sort of updated miner's headlamp. I stretched its elastic band around my head until its compact light rested on my forehead like a third eye.

"Stylish," I said, getting to my feet.

I'd complained about bedtime as a matter of principle, but actually I was looking forward to bed. As we walked through the arched doorway into the concentrated darkness of the treehouse, I switched on my headlamp and aimed it at the three bunks. Being grown-ups, Mom and Dad had picked the bottom one. Tilley wanted the middle to be close to Mom and Dad, so I got the top. I climbed eight feet up the wooden ladder and clambered onto my brand new foam mattress. On top of my quilt lay the green garbage bag that contained my entire wardrobe. There wasn't much space to put my clothes away. My bunk had three drawers underneath, sort of like a captain's bed. Like a lot of old wooden drawers, though, they were hard to open. I filled two of them but the third was jammed shut. I gave up on trying to open it and hung the rest of my clothes on the hooks that we'd screwed into the oak branches at either end of the bunks.

We had put curtains around the bunks to make them all private, like the sleeping berths of trains. I pulled my curtain shut. I had enough headroom to sit up, so I changed the normal way into my pyjama top. Pants required a special method. I lay down, lifted my butt, wriggled my shorts to my knees, sat back down and pulled the shorts over my feet. Pyjama bottoms went on the same way, in reverse order.

Before hanging up my shorts I took out my wallet and removed the torn blue strip of the letter we'd found in the stream. Maybe, I thought, Great-great-aunt Lydia is one of those people who can't say anything at all unless they can think of the perfect way to say it. Maybe she'd ripped up the letter because its welcome didn't quite match the welcome in her heart. Maybe it seemed too inky and papery compared to the welcome that she really wanted to give. I thought this was the best theory so far. I put the torn blue strip back in my wallet, and shut it in the little cupboard above my bunk. "Goodnight," I called. I got under my quilt and switched off my headlamp.

That night I realized that what I'd always thought of as silence had actually been the buzz of the fridge and the hum of faraway traffic. The same thing for darkness. My street-lit version of darkness at the apartment was nothing compared to this. In my bunk I couldn't see my own hand, not even when I touched it to my nose. The pure silence and total darkness of the treehouse were new to me. It was actually fascinating to see and hear absolutely nothing. I listened to the silence and I watched the darkness for as long as I could manage to stay awake.

NOTEBOOK: #5

NAME: Rosamund McGrady

SUBJECT: The Code

Bird twitters woke me up.

I propped up on my elbow to look out the round porthole window above my pillow. There was a nest on the oak branch, and a yellow-crested something swept in for a landing. Baby birds raised their fluffy heads and I watched the yellow-crested mother dangle breakfast worms down their throats. Then I got up. It was my first day of living at the treehouse, and I had things to do.

I stuck my head out from my bunk curtains. Below me, Mom and Dad and Tilley sat eating Cheerios at the folding table. Mom and Dad were eating them out of bowls; Tilley was threading hers onto a string, then letting them slide down into her mouth. On our camping stove a coffee pot blurped out nice coffee smells.

"There she is," Mom said, blowing me a morning kiss. "Better get some breakfast. We've got to go soon."

"'*We*' as in you and Dad, right?" I asked. I knew that

Mom and Dad had to go to their summer jobs at the university. Dad's job was to count the live bugs and the dead bugs in a huge glass case and put the results on a chart. Mom's job was to make computerized voice-graphs out of tape-recorded animal noises.

"'*We*' as in all four of us," Dad said.

"Where are Tilley and I going?" I asked, but my sinking heart already knew the answer. We were going to the University Childhood Development Centre drop-in day camp. Every single summer of our lives Mom and Dad had taken Tilley and me to the University Childhood Development Centre drop-in day camp. I had hoped that this summer would be different.

"To day camp," Dad said. "Where else?"

"Not day camp!" I said. "Please spare me day camp. Please, O merciful one!"

"What's wrong with day camp?"

"What's *wrong* with day camp? Like, everything! They make us do a bunch of stupid crafts, like making caterpillars out of egg cartons. Five days a week. Eight hours straight. It's like being in some child labour factory." I thought hard for the worst thing I could say. "It's unstimulating."

"The University Childhood Development Centre is unstimulating?" Dad asked.

"Totally. I can actually feel my left brain shrinking in that day camp room," I claimed. "Couldn't we just stay here and, um, study the ecosystems of the meadow and stream and stuff? I can look after myself, you know. I'm practically twelve. I can look after Tilley, too."

"I don't know, Rosie," Dad said.

"I hate the way you think that if we're not supervised every second we're going to throw ourselves into traffic, or make friends with weirdos or something." I searched my mind for the right buzz words. "It lowers my self-esteem."

"And there's no traffic here," Tilley pointed out.

"No weirdos either," I said. Mom wasn't saying anything, so I guessed she was on my side. I had an inspiration. "How can you expect us to develop any sense of responsibility when you won't give us any responsibility?"

Dad and Mom looked at each other. "We'll obey all your rules," I persisted. "We'll use common sense. We'll be on our best behaviour. We'll be mature for our ages. We'll be. . . ." I paused to think.

"Good," Tilley supplied.

"Good," I agreed.

"Maybe we could give it a try, David," Mom said, and then they both recited rule after rule, as if they were getting paid for each one they could think up. No playing with matches. No playing with camping fuel. No playing with propane. No approaching raccoons. No feeding raccoons. No enabling raccoons to feed themselves. No leaving garbage where raccoons can get it. No leaving the treehouse with an open door, or with a window opened wider than a raccoon. No riding in the dumbwaiter. No horseplay on the ladder. And for Tilley, no climbing to or from the treehouse unless I was on the ladder below. (The idea, I guess, was that I could catch her as she hurtled toward me like a meteor.) On and on, the rules went.

"Okay, got them," I said. "Got the rules. Okay, so Tilley and I will clean up. You guys go off to work." I wanted them gone before they could think up any more rules, or, worse, change their minds about leaving us alone. I watched until Mom and Dad disappeared through the trap door in the porch, and then I just stood there awhile, experiencing the feel of myself alone in my new home. "I guess I better do the dishes," I said, listening to the responsibility vibrate in my voice.

I squeezed dish soap into the plastic washbasin and carried it to the pump on the porch. I pumped the handle until my arms ached, then Tilley pumped for a bit, then me again, then Tilley again, then me again. I was thinking that our plumbing system had failed when the water finally gushed out of the spout, all over my runners. After swishing the bowls and mugs through the suds I turned them upside down on the porch boards to dry. When I threw the dishwater over the porch banister, blue jays swooped from the oak branches and flew off with the soggy Cheerios. "Okay Tilley," I said. "Let's explore."

On that first day of freedom, we discovered about a gazillion cool things. We found a little island in the stream, with a snowball bush in blossom. The stream was full of little see-through fish, all darting around in one big school and failing to think for themselves. We ran back to the treehouse for a saucepan to fish with. They were innocent, unsuspicious fish, and easy to catch. In the meadow we found fluorescent green grasshoppers. The grasshoppers were smarter than the fish. We had to sneak up to catch those.

Our grasshopper hunt brought us further and further across the meadow, all the way to the stable near the stone wall that separated the Grand Oak estate from Bellemonde Drive. It was a fancy stable, sort of a miniature Grand Oak Manor for horses. But there were no horses, we saw as we flattened our noses against the dusty window. There was only an old car with a running board and a winged hood ornament. "A Bentley," I said, because I know my hood ornaments. From the stable, Tilley and I followed the little hedge that enclosed the Manor and its garden. The Manor garden was all formal and manicured, not at all like the tousled meadow on the other side. The hedge was so short that I could have jumped over without even taking a run at it, but one of Mom and Dad's rules was that we couldn't go inside the hedge without an actual invitation. I wasn't about to violate any rules and find myself imprisoned in day camp, so Tilley and I just looked over the hedge at the paths that wound through the Manor garden. We saw birds splashing in a birdbath, and we saw the random flight patterns of yellow butterflies, but we saw no sign of human life. "Where do you think Great-great-aunt Lydia is all the time?" I asked.

"Inside her mansion," Tilley guessed. I thought so too.

At lunchtime Tilley and I climbed back to the treehouse to get crackers and cheese. We were going to eat them in the cherry orchard in the meadow, along with cherries for a balanced diet. The crackers had not yet been unpacked, and Tilley drifted around the treehouse as I looked for them. "Hey," Tilley said as I knelt rummaging in a box. "Look what I found." She held out a paper. It was the exact same blue as the torn strip of letter from the stream.

"What? Where?"

"In here," Tilley stuck her finger inside a hollow knothole in one of the huge oak branches that cut through the six corners of our treehouse. "Right here, in this little cave in the branch."

I took the blue paper from her hand and unfolded it.

*From the Desk of*
*Lydia Florence Augustine McGrady*
*Grand Oak Manor*
*Number 9 Bellemonde Drive*

ID ID NO TE VERTHIN KAPA IROFSCIS SORSCO ULDDO SOMU CHHARM. IHA VETOLE AVETH ISBLO ODYHO USE.
ABADDES TIN YAWA ITS MEHERE.
ALI FEISSOE ASI LYL OST.
LE TUSESCA PE. LE TUSELO PE.
I SOB ELME ETME: THETRE EHO US EATTEN.

X

"It's on Great-great-aunt Lydia's stationery," I told Tilley. She was just out of kindergarten and couldn't read cursive yet. As she looked at the block letters though, she moved her lips to sound out the words. "What does Great-great-aunt Lydia say?" Tilley asked, giving up.

"I don't know. It's in code."

"Let's uncode it."

"Decode it. Yeah. I'll do that while you pick the cherries."

Pen and paper in hand, I headed across the meadow and climbed one of the gnarled cherry trees. Settling onto a branch, I stared at Great-great-aunt Lydia's coded letter. My best clue for cracking the code was the final letter, 'X', where the signature would normally be. That had to be an

'L', for Lydia. So if 'X' was code for 'L', that meant the code alphabet was twelve letters ahead of the real alphabet. I wrote out the two alphabets.

| | | | |
|---|---|---|---|
| A=M | H=T | O=A | V=H |
| B=N | I=U | P=B | W=I |
| C=O | J=V | Q=C | X=J |
| D=P | K=W | R=D | Y=K |
| E=Q | L=X | S=E | Z=L |
| F=R | M=Y | T=F | |
| G=S | N=Z | U=G | |

Then I started decoding. WR WR BC HS JSFHVWB was what I got for the first five words. It made no sense.

Tilley climbed down to my branch, dangling cherries from her fingers. "What does it say?" she asked. Cherries dangled from her ears too.

"This is harder than I thought," I said. "I'll figure it out later."

"Okay," Tilley said. "I bet I can spit cherry pits farther than you."

"We'll see about that." I curled my tongue into a blowgun and spat my cherry pit. It shot a respectable distance over the meadow. Tilley spat her cherry pit. It went a really long way. She had a natural advantage at spitting because of her missing front teeth. "Good one," I said.

"That code letter is on the same blue paper as the ripped-up letter you found in the stream," Tilley observed.

"Yeah," I said. "The exact same blue."

"And Great-great-aunt Lydia's name is at the top of

the code letter, right?"

"Yeah. It's her stationery."

"And that means Great-great-aunt Lydia wrote both letters, right?" Tilley spat another long-distance cherry pit.

"Right."

"How come she rips stuff up, and writes stuff in code? How come she doesn't want us to read what she writes?"

I ate a triplet of cherries while I considered. Then I spat the three pits one after another, like semi-automatic gunfire. "Maybe she's testing us. Maybe she has a secret that she doesn't want to tell unless we prove ourselves worthy. Maybe she wants to find out if we're smart enough to share her special knowledge."

"What kind of special knowledge?"

"That's what we've got to figure out," I said.

"So Great-great-aunt Lydia's not like other grown-ups, right?"

"Right. She's eccentric."

"What's eccentric mean?"

"Eccentric? Eccentric means weird," I said. "Weird in a good way."

NOTEBOOK: #6

NAME: Rosamund McGrady

SUBJECT: The Pleasure of Her Company

Great-great-aunt Lydia's letter was harder to decode than I'd expected. Every night at bedtime I'd pull the curtain shut around my bunk and read it with my headlamp. I experimented. I wrote out the normal alphabet with possible code alphabets beside it. I tried a code alphabet starting with 'B'. I tried one starting with 'C'. I tried one starting with every possible letter. None of it was right. Sometimes I'd also get out the torn blue strip that we'd found in the stream, and I'd put it beside the coded letter, and I'd stare at both papers as if their mystery would solve itself, like one of those optical illusion pictures where you stare and stare and can't see the old lady's face, and then suddenly you can. But it never worked. Every night I'd give up and turn off my headlamp, and lie in the dark wondering about Great-great-aunt Lydia.

Weeks had gone by without any other sign of her. She didn't leave any more flowers and she didn't leave any more notes. She didn't appear in person, either, even though Tilley and I were constantly on the lookout, wherever we were.

The whole of July, Tilley and I almost never left the grounds of Grand Oak Manor for the outside world. It was a long way to walk. We'd sold our car and bought bikes instead, but with Tilley on training wheels even the ride seemed long, and then when we reached the outside world, it was all normal and boring anyway, with its sidewalks and streetlights and parked SUVs. Tilley and I rode once to the community centre to wash our hair in the showers of the swimming pool changing room, but it was unrewarding. On the ride back to the treehouse we decided to start cleaning ourselves in the stream instead. We found a deep spot upstream, and we made it deeper by damming it with river rocks. It was a lot of work. When Mom and Dad saw our dam I was afraid they'd say that we had abused our riparian rights, or something, but they were actually pleased, and impressed by our engineering.

"But no soap or shampoo, not even biodegradable," said Dad. "We don't want to give Great-great-aunt Lydia anything to complain about." It was a constant concern of Dad's, that we not give Great-great-aunt Lydia anything to complain about. We were very careful. Our garbage, for example, we bundled up like a baby every morning and tucked into our bike trailer. Dad transported it to the university for proper disposal. Our outhouse is another example of how careful we were. Instead of making an ordinary one we made an environmentally friendly composting toilet. We all had to dig and dig, even Tilley, because Mom and Dad had taken me seriously when I'd said we needed responsibility. It was worth the effort, though, because our composting toilet was so environmentally amazing that Mom and Dad actually got a government grant for making it. As scientists, Mom and Dad are skilled at getting government grants. Tilley thought it was hilarious that the government was paying us to study our own toilet.

Because of the toilet grant, we also got a city permit to occupy the treehouse as a research station. When Dad climbed through the trap door onto the porch after his trip to City Hall, he held up the printed green permit for all of us to see. "There you go," he said. "Now we're completely legal."

Because of Dad's determination to be totally legal, we didn't have any campfires our first month at the treehouse. City by-laws forbid open fires on residential property. However, Mom and Dad's friend Clarkson researched a loophole. On July 23 he told us that Grand Oak was an exception to the by-law. The grounds of Grand Oak Manor were so big that they counted as rural acreage, and therefore open fires were allowed. We made a big campfire that night to celebrate. Campfires became my passion. After Clarkson's legal opinion, I made one every single night.

One evening late in July, Mom and Dad came riding home to the bald patch of ground by the stream where I was just starting our nightly campfire. Dropping her bike, Mom asked the same question that she asked every night. "Any sign of Great-great-aunt Lydia?"

I was down on my knees, blowing into my teepee of kindling. "Mom," I said. "As if I wouldn't mention it."

"Still not, eh," Mom said. She sat on a stump beside me. "Well, you know, I think it's time somebody broke the ice. I think we should invite her for dinner."

"How are we going to invite her to dinner?" Dad asked, getting off his own bike. "She's a senior citizen. She's not going to want to scramble up that ladder to the treehouse."

"Dinner doesn't have to be *in* the treehouse," Mom said. "We could entertain her down here on the ground. Do what we're doing tonight. Make a campfire. Roast hot dogs. Marshmallows."

"I don't know if that's Great-great-aunt Lydia's style," Dad said, putting his bike down.

"We don't know her style one way or another," Mom said. "But we could do something fancier, if you think that's better. Rosie's birthday is coming up. We could have a party."

I liked this idea. I had been warned not to expect a birthday party this year because:

a) Most of our cash had gone to fix up the treehouse, and we had to really watch our spending until Mom and Dad got their new student loans in September;
b) All my friends lived across town, and it would be hard to get them to the treehouse. (I thought this was a lame reason, for people as resourceful as we were.); and
c) I was going to be twelve years old, and was therefore, according to Mom and Dad, too mature for birthday parties. I felt a pang when

> they told me this, but I didn't want to argue that I was not too mature.

"I think inviting Great-great-aunt Lydia is an excellent idea," I said. If we invited her, we'd buy lots of treat food. Plus, she would give me a really good present. Something worthy of a rich, eccentric aunt. Something expensive and unusual. But mainly, I was curious to meet her.

"I don't know," Dad said.

Suddenly I thought of something. I got the torn blue strip from my wallet.

"Great-great-aunt Lydia wanted to invite *us*," I said. "That's what she means by 'ation fo someday soon'. I think she's talking about an *invit*ation someday soon."

Dad took the torn letter, then handed it back. "Lots of words end with 'ation,'" he said. "And if she wanted to give an invitation, she wouldn't have ripped it up."

"I know!" I said. "She wanted *us* to invite *her*. *She* was hoping for an invitation someday soon. But then she realized that wasn't polite, and that's why she ripped the letter up! And she's been hoping to hear from us ever since. And she'll be so, so, so happy to get invited to my birthday party!"

"I don't know," Dad said again. "So far she isn't making any trouble for us. Maybe we should leave well enough alone."

"You think a birthday party invitation is going to cause her to make trouble for us?" Mom asked. "And your reasoning is . . . ?"

"Out of sight, out of mind," Dad shrugged. "If she comes face to face with us, she might decide to drive us out."

"Why would she decide that?"

"Because of a long history of family conflict."

"Family conflict that doesn't involve you or me or the girls. Family conflict from years before we were even born. Honestly, David, I don't know why you insist on thinking of her as an enemy! She's a lonely old lady living all by herself with no family of her own. She'll fall in love with the girls at first sight. One look at how cute they are and that family conflict will be history. She'll be serving them tea in the turret three times a week."

"You really think so," Dad said.

"I really do."

"Okay." Dad sighed, but he seemed careful not to sigh too hard. "So we'll invite her." He picked up the axe and began chopping wood.

We planned my birthday party as we roasted hot dogs over the campfire. "We should send a written invitation," Mom said, rotating her alder twig to brown her hot dog evenly. "That's more respectful than telephone." After dinner, Mom got a pen and paper and returned to the campfire. As the rest of us toasted marshmallows she wrote a letter requesting the pleasure of Great-great-aunt Lydia's company. At the bottom she put RSVP.

"What's my cell number, Rosie?" Mom asked. "I guess I should know, but I never give it out, and I never call myself."

I had to think for a moment, because most of my calls to Mom were through the speed-dial on Dad's cell. I told her and she wrote it down and folded the letter into the envelope. In her very best handwriting she addressed the envelope to Miss Lydia Florence Augustine McGrady, Grand Oak Manor, Number 9 Bellemonde Drive.

We talked about how to deliver it. We couldn't get to her front door mail slot without either trespassing through the Manor garden, or scaling the stone wall that separated the estate grounds from Bellemonde Drive. Neither seemed like a good idea, so the next day Mom and Dad brought the invitation to the university, and mailed it back to the estate they'd just come from.

I was impatient for Great-great-aunt Lydia's reply. "Check your voice mail," I kept telling Mom, but whenever she did there was still no message from Great-great-aunt Lydia. "We did give her the right number, didn't we," Mom asked as she checked her voice mail three days before the party.

"Yeah," I said, and I recited it.

Mom pushed buttons on her phone. "I hate to tell you this, Rosie," she said, "but that's *not* my phone number. You switched the seven and the nine."

"I did?"

"You did."

"Oh no. Oh Mom. I'm sorry."

"It's okay, Rosie," Mom said. "She knows where to find us. I'm sure if she wasn't coming, she'd get a message to us somehow."

We carried on with the party plans. In preparation for Great-great-aunt Lydia, we built a stone fire ring, to reassure her that we were not about to set her grounds ablaze. We rolled a hollow stump from far away in the woods, and chopped it into an armchair for her.

Two days before my birthday, Mom said "I guess we'd better go order a birthday cake." We had a long tradition of homemade birthday cakes, with amateur rosettes and crooked writing and crumbs in the icing, but the treehouse had no oven. Mom and I set off on our bikes to custom-order a professional cake. After locking our bikes in the supermarket parking lot we went to the bakery counter. "My *God* these are expensive!" Mom declared. She sounded insulted. "And big! Look at that one, it must be a tenth of an acre! We'd only eat a corner. We couldn't even fit the leftovers in our fridge. No, forget this." Argument did not change Mom's mind. We left the supermarket, cakeless.

The next afternoon Mom made an oven by tenting scrap aluminum over the fire ring, and she baked a birthday cake over the evening fire. Bits of ash stuck in the batter, and when the cake was turned out of the pan we saw that the bottom had been burned to pure black carbon. Knowing Mom, I expected her to say that it would be perfectly fine once it was iced. She didn't though. Sensibly, she threw the whole cake onto the embers, like the chunk of fuel it was already well on its way to becoming.

The next day the sound of hammering woke me up. "Happy Birthday," Tilley yelled when I peered out from my bunk curtain. She came up the bunk ladder with a present flopping in its gift-wrap. Mom and Dad stood with their coffee mugs, watching me open it. I unwrapped slowly to draw out the experience. I reached into the loosened wrapping. It was . . . a fleece jacket. "A fleece jacket," I exclaimed. I was exclaiming falsely, from pure politeness. This was a disappointing present.

"It's kind of a practical present," Dad apologized.

"But we have something else that's not so sensible," Mom said.

"And you're gonna really like it." Tilley tugged my pyjama sleeve. "Come and see!"

She led me out on the porch and pointed at the branch that rose through the trap door. Our ladder no longer ended at porch level: new wooden rungs continued up the branch and disappeared into the oak leaves above.

"My present is up there?" I asked.

Tilley nodded at high speed. "Go up," she urged.

I climbed up the angled branch. Out beyond the porch banister I glanced down, and the distance between my top-stitched running shoe and the meadow was shocking. I made myself continue. This birthday ladder went higher and higher, and further and further out, until I reached a plywood platform. I climbed onto it. Behind and below me was the treehouse roof, which I'd never seen before. In front of me was a rope that hung from a higher branch. "Pull up the rope," my family yelled from their cluster on the porch.

Hand over hand I reeled it in, watching it coil up on the platform. The rope seemed to go on forever, but finally I reached a plywood disk on a big knot.

"It's a swing!" Tilley shouted out. I'd been afraid of that.

"Give it a try," called Mom.

They had not been kidding when they said this present was not so sensible. This present was insane. *What are you thinking?* I wanted to shout down at my family. Are you the same parents who always forbade swimming until after one full hour of digestion? The ones who never let me run with a popsicle? The ones who kept the cough syrup and plant food in a padlocked cupboard? And now that I've survived twelve years, you try to kill me?

"You're not scared, are you sweetie?" Mom asked.

"Go Rosie! It's so fun,"Tilley called.

"Just hang on tight and you'll be fine," Dad called. "Really."

I tucked the disk between my legs, and then I just stood there for a long time, holding the rope and taking in the aerial view of the meadow. Jump, I kept telling myself. Sometimes I felt such a rush of determination that for a split second I'd think I actually *had* jumped, and then I'd realize that I was still just standing there on the branch. Then I did jump. I was surprised I'd done it, and I was sorry too. There was a long, sickening free fall. Then the rope snapped tight and I flew out across the meadow. Speed stretched my cheeks backward. Branches and clouds zipped around. I zoomed to the sky and hung in mid-air for a moment. Then I dropped and swung backward, my brain and stomach left behind in the rush. Then forward again, then backward, over and over, in arcs that were a bit smaller each time. When the swing was almost still, I jumped to the ground. It was the best birthday present I'd ever had.

Tilley and I spent most of the day on the rope swing. In the hot part of the afternoon we splashed around in our dammed-up pool. At five we got dressed and helped with party preps. By seven we were all set. The tree-stump armchair was nicely padded with all four of our bunk pillows. The table, made from a plank borrowed from our bridge, was set with a bedsheet tablecloth and a bouquet of flowers picked from the meadow. Nine shish kebabs were threaded onto alder twigs, ready for roasting. The vegetable plate was artistically arranged under a veil of plastic wrap, and so was the fruit. Bottles of root beer chilled in the stream, and a bottle of white wine too. There was nothing left to do but wait for Great-great-aunt Lydia, who was due any minute.

We tried not to wait too hard. We tried talking, but our sentences kept drifting into thin air, and our gazes kept drifting toward Grand Oak Manor. The meadow and the lawn and the mansion stayed as still as a poster. We watched the landscape for Great-great-aunt Lydia. Our expectation was so intense that at the first flicker of movement I nearly yelled that it was her, before I realized that what I saw was a coyote, three feet tall, with four legs and a tail.

At seven-thirty Mom uncapped the root beer. At eight she removed the plastic wrap. Eventually we lit the fire, and as the darkness settled we roasted the shish kebabs. No one sat in the comfy tree-stump armchair, which seemed occupied by Great-great-aunt Lydia's absence. I tried to pretend that I was not disappointed that she hadn't come. My birthday cake substitute was s'mores, but for Great-great-aunt Lydia alone, Mom had bought a single chocolate éclair. She and Dad took turns eating it. "I'm sure she wanted to come," Mom said, swallowing her half of the éclair. "I can feel it. Something's prevented her." Dad said nothing.

It's impossible to stick birthday candles into graham wafers, so we tucked them into little paper boats, one for each year. Mom lit the candles as Tilley launched the boats. The three of them sang 'Happy Birthday' into the pure darkness. I watched the tiny lights wiggle down the black stream, chased by the shimmer of their reflections. "Make a wish as the last candle disappears," Dad said. "New tradition." I did.

I wished super hard, the way you're supposed to for wishes to come true.

As we were returning to the campfire I looked up to see eyes glinting in the distance. "Quick, the flashlight, who's got it?" I whispered, but by the time I lit up the darkness, the eyes had gone.

We stayed at the campfire until Tilley's eyelids began to close. As we climbed the ladder to the treehouse, stars spangled between the leaves. By headlamp, I got ready for bed, draping my clothes onto the loaded hook at the foot of my bunk. They hung there dutifully for a moment, then slid to the floor. I climbed down the bunk ladder to get them and on my way back up, I pulled on my jammed drawer.

For once, it slid open. As I went to stuff my clothes inside, something glinted in the thin beam of my headlamp. I reached into the dark drawer and felt a pair of scissors. As I drew them out I saw they weren't ordinary scissors at all. They had gold handles in the shape of a bird, with long, silver blades for the beak. I brought them close and read the engraving. LFAMcG. Lydia Florence Augustine McGrady. The handles said 18 k, for eighteen karat gold. The silver blades were skewed, but they were razor sharp. The scissors were beautiful.

For me, I thought. Eccentric Great-great-aunt Lydia had given me a birthday present after all. An expensive one, and an unusual one, just like I'd hoped for. There was no birthday card, but I wouldn't expect one from her. Great-great-aunt Lydia did not believe in using the plain Hallmark language of birthday cards. Great-great-aunt Lydia believed in communicating by more mysterious methods.

I climbed into my bunk with the scissors, thinking that it was quite cool that Great-great-aunt Lydia had managed to sneak up to the treehouse on my birthday and put them in my drawer. I put the scissors in my bunk cupboard and turned off my headlamp. Exhausted, I nestled onto my pillow and felt my happy birthday thoughts dissolving into sleep. But a new thought flung my eyelids open. Why did I think that Great-great-aunt Lydia had put the scissors in the drawer that day? Could Great-great-aunt Lydia even make it up the ladder to the treehouse? I had never opened that drawer before: the scissors could have been there all along.

But the drawer had opened easily, and it had always been jammed before. Therefore, hadn't someone been in the treehouse, unjamming it? Or had I just finally discovered the right way to open it? I'd never tried the drawer from the ladder before.

But did it make any sense that the scissors had been there all along? Great-great-aunt Lydia wouldn't have just abandoned eighteen karat gold scissors in the treehouse, would she? The scissors had to be there as a present, I concluded. A birthday present for me.

But if the scissors were a birthday present, then why hadn't Great-great-aunt Lydia come to my party? Maybe she was shy? So shy that she'd lost the nerve to deliver the letter she'd written us on moving day, and ripped it up. So shy that she could only communicate through secret codes in hidden places.

I lay in the dense darkness, trying to figure it all out. I was too sleepy to reach a conclusion. But just like Mom, I had a good feeling about Great-great-aunt Lydia. I had a feeling that sooner or later, we were going to be friends.

NOTEBOOK: #7

NAME: Rosamund McGrady

SUBJECT: The Lady of the Manor

The day we encountered Great-great-aunt Lydia started off like any other summer day.

The morning sun beamed heat rays. Like a magnifying glass, the round porthole window above my bunk focussed them on the back of my neck. I woke up just as I was about to burst into flames. It seemed like it anyway. I flung back my sheet and got out of the treehouse.

Tilley was already out on the porch, drawing fake bruises on herself with markers. The two of us wandered to the blackberry bushes that grew against Great-great-aunt Lydia's stone wall and filled up an empty yogourt container. We ate our blackberries lying in the meadow, with ants running over our legs.

"This is my best bruise," Tilley said, pointing to a horrific expanse of purplish flesh above her knee.

"Yeah," I said. "It's great. It looks totally real. You could probably get a job drawing bruises on actors."

"Really?" Tilley seemed thrilled. "I can teach you how to do them. You have to smudge in the green and the yellow in my secret way."

"Okay. Show me after breakfast."

We'd brought along breakfast cookies to go with the blackberries. They were chocolate chip oatmeal, from a package. We felt lucky to have packaged cookies. For awhile, Mom had been making homemade ones in her experimental campfire oven and Tilley and I were afraid that those charred pucks were the only cookies we'd ever get. Fortunately, though, Mom is a good enough scientist to know when an experiment has failed.

A crumb of my store-bought cookie fell to the meadow. Tilley and I watched an ant make off with it. "I bet the ant really likes it," Tilley said.

"I bet," I said, taking another bite. "He'll probably spend the rest of his life searching the meadow for more."

Tilley crumbled some of her cookie over the meadow. "There," she said. "Now he won't be sad."

After breakfast, Tilley lay in the meadow making daisy chains while I tried again to decode Great-great-aunt Lydia's letter. I tried the alphabet backward. I tried writing the first thirteen letters of the alphabet, with the remaining letters underneath, and switching each letter with the one above or below. Then I tried writing the top thirteen letters backward. Then I tried writing the bottom thirteen backward. Then my brain began to hurt. I folded the coded letter back in my wallet.

"Time for bike practice," I said. As I mentioned, we'd sold our car. A car is not very useful when you can't drive it to your home. Bikes were now our main transportation, so it was important that Tilley progress beyond training wheels. I got the bikes from our prefab garden shed and wheeled them to the meadow. Again and again I ran beside Tilley, providing moral and physical support until she wobbled off on her brief solos. Afterwards, we cooled off in our dammed pool, and lay in the meadow to dry.

"Let's visit Oscar," Tilley said. Oscar was Tilley's name for the crayfish who lived in the shadow of a big rock upstream. Tilley considered Oscar a pet, and was very affectionate with him. She would scoop him up from the stream bed and baby talk to him and stroke his armored back. Oscar never showed any affection in return. I was not actually convinced that Oscar was only one crayfish. He seemed to be slightly different sizes and colours on different days.

Once we'd returned Oscar to his natural habitat, Tilley and I raced leaves down the stream. This is not as childish as it sounds. We didn't throw our leaves in just any old place. We studied the currents carefully. We learned about undertows that could suck leaves beneath the surface, and about backwaters that could strand leaves into making slow circles forever and ever. We learned about rapids that could shipwreck leaves on rock islands. We became experts in hydro-kinetic theory.

When we got tired of racing leaves, we took the path into Great-great-aunt Lydia's woods and gathered kindling for the nightly campfire. We were heading, arms full, back toward the treehouse when Tilley stopped on the plank bridge. "Rosie," she said, turning toward me. "A lady."

Looking across the meadow to Grand Oak Manor, I saw two men by the hedge. One man wore overalls and looked like a workman. The other man wore a cardigan and a tie, and he looked like, maybe, a supervisor. He was standing with his arms crossed, watching the workman work. It took me a second to see the lady. She was off by herself, on a second storey balcony. She had pale blue hair that must have been hairsprayed, because it was as stiff as a new pad of steel wool. She was standing very still. Beside her was a basset hound, also very still.

"It's Great-great-aunt Lydia!" Tilley said. "Let's get invited for tea!" She dropped her kindling and ran, stopping at the hedge underneath the balcony. "Great-great-aunt Lydia!" Tilley waved the way you'd wave at a plane if you were stranded on a desert island. "Hi! Hi, Great-great-aunt Lydia! Hi! Hi!"

Tilley stopped waving to think of a more formal introduction. "How do you do," she yelled at the top of her lungs. "I'm your great-great-niece? Matilda? Her too! She's Rosamund! Pleased to meet you!" Slowly Great-great-aunt Lydia looked down at Tilley. Her face was expressionless. Tilley looked very little and bruised, standing there by the hedge.

Great-great-aunt Lydia didn't say anything to Tilley. She flipped open a cell phone. She called the supervisor man. I heard his phone ringing in his corner of the hedge. His ring tone was *In the Hall of the Mountain King* by Edvard Grieg. I know because we studied it in Grade Six Music (the whole song, not the ring tone). The supervisor man flipped his phone to his ear. He talked and put it back in his pocket. Then he bent down and picked up something flat and square from the lawn of the Manor garden.

I was just starting to figure out what the workman was

making. At the corners of the hedge were new, tall posts and I guessed they were for a fence. The supervisor man handed the flat, square thing to the workman, and the workman hammered it on the post. It was a sign.

"SSSS," Tilley said. Being just out of kindergarten, she didn't know how to read yet, but she did know her letters. She struggled to sound out the words.

"SSSSSTTTTT" Tilley ventured.

What the sign said was *Stay Off—Private Property*.

I walked up to Tilley and tugged her hand. "Come on, Tilley," I said. I didn't think we'd be going for tea at Grand Oak Manor any time soon.

| | |
|---|---|
| NOTEBOOK: | #8 |
| NAME: | Rosamund McGrady |
| SUBJECT: | Trespassers Will Be Prosecuted |

The workman was at Grand Oak Manor again the next morning. Through the treehouse walls we heard him sawing, and from the treehouse porch, we glimpsed him through the oak leaves.

"I wonder what he's doing now," I said.

"Let's spy on him," said Tilley. Her six-year-old ambition was to be a spy when she grew up. "Let's do secret spy stuff."

We decided that the snowball bush on the island would be a good spy station. With a backpack of spy supplies, we climbed down from the treehouse and sauntered toward it, glancing sideways at the workman. While he was bent over his saw, we waded to the island and ducked inside the bush. If he noticed, when he straightened up, that we had suddenly disappeared from the landscape, he didn't show it. We made ourselves comfortable in the spattered green shade. I opened my backpack and got out the high-powered binoculars that Dad used to observe insect life. Parting the snowball blossoms, I aimed the binoculars at the workman and set the power to maximum.

"Wow, are these ever strong," I said. "I can see all his pores!"

"What's he doing?" Tilley asked.

"Can't tell. I can only see his nose and upper lip. Hang on, I'm switching to low power. Okay, that's better. Here," I said, handing the binoculars to Tilley. "You can have the first turn." This made her happy, because she was all thrilled with the idea of spying, but I had guessed that there were going to be a lot of slow times. As one of our spying supplies, I'd brought along a library book on cryptography to keep myself busy.

"He's doing the boards now," Tilley said, when I was halfway through the chapter on transposition ciphers. "He's putting them up and down."

"Oh. Yeah?" I said without looking up. The book was making me think Great-great-aunt Lydia might have replaced the normal alphabet with a keyword code. A keyword code is an alphabet that starts with a secret word, followed by the remaining letters of the alphabet. I wrote out the real alphabet, and under it I wrote LYDIABCEFGHJKMNOPQRSTUVWXZ.

"He just nailed another board," Tilley reported a minute later. "He's putting them so we can't climb them. Look." She shoved the binoculars at me.

I took them and poked the lenses through the blossoms. "Wow! Pretty high! She's not fooling around, is she?"

"Why is she doing that?" Tilley asked. "Is it because she's really, really, really shy? Like you said before?"

"Nope," I said. "Shy would be if she wanted to be friends but was too scared. A big fence means she doesn't want to be friends at all." It hurt my heart to say it. From the moment I saw the *Stay Off—Private Property* sign the day before, I'd been missing the Great-great-aunt Lydia I'd first imagined. It was weird of me, I knew, to miss someone I had basically made up. Get over your imaginary friend, I told myself. But I couldn't help being disappointed by the real Great-great-aunt Lydia, out of sight somewhere on the other side of her unfinished fence.

"Why doesn't she want to be friends?" Tilley asked.

"I don't know. She's hard to figure out."

I began translating Great-great-aunt Lydia's coded letter from the 'Lydia' keyword code. DC DC OP UH WHSUKDO, was what I got for the first five words. Wrong again.

"Here comes that guy in the cardigan," Tilley said. "He's got another sign. Now he's handing it to the carpenter guy. Now the carpenter guy's nailing it to the fence. It's got a 'B' in it, and then it's got an 'E' in it, and then it's got a 'W'. . . ."

I snatched the binoculars. "Beware," I read out loud. "Guard Dog On Duty."

"Does she mean that dog with the dragging stomach? That dog didn't bark or growl or anything."

"No, he wasn't too excitable," I said.

"Maybe she has a meaner dog in the mansion."

"Maybe. Or maybe she's pretending about the guard dog to keep us out," I said, passing the binoculars back to Tilley. I was determined to crack Great-great-aunt Lydia's code. I tried McGrady as a keyword, but that didn't work either. 'Florence' couldn't be the keyword, because there was more than one 'E', and 'Augustine' couldn't either, for the same reason, two 'U's.

"Okay, so now the guy in the cardigan's holding another sign," Tilley said. I held out my hand for the binoculars. *Keep Out*, the sign said. *Trespassers Will Be Prosecuted.*

"You know how our great-great-grandfather, Magnus, gave everything to Great-great-aunt Lydia?" Tilley said as the day wore on. "And nothing to Great-grampa? How come he did that? Wasn't Great-grampa nice?"

I wasn't sure I really remembered Great-grampa. I had an image of his crooked smile, but was that a memory or just a photo from our album? "Yeah, he was nice," I guessed.

"So why was that Magnus person so mad at him?"

"Maybe Great-great-aunt Lydia poisoned his mind against Great-grampa."

"Like, tattled on him?"

"Yeah, tattled big time," I said. "Probably for something he didn't even do."

"So Great-great-aunt Lydia is mean, right?"

"Right."

"Not weird in a good way."

"Nope."

"Why did she bring us flowers then?"

"Well, she smashed them up. As a symbol. To mean the total opposite of welcome."

"That's *so* mean."

"Yup."

"Well, why did she write that letter and then rip it up?"

"I don't know," I admitted.

"'Cause doesn't she say forgive and welcome and stuff? And an invitation someday soon?"

I opened my wallet and got out the torn blue strip. "Maybe she's saying she'll *never* forgive, and we're *not* welcome. Who knows? And it doesn't say 'invitation'. Just 'ation'. It could be, I don't know, an *explan*ation someday soon. *Inform*ation someday soon. *Communic*ation someday soon."

"Maybe she means that letter you're uncoding."

"Maybe."

"What do you think that code letter says?" Tilley asked. "Like, what do you think it's about?"

"Probably about the big split in the family. And probably about whatever is her big problem with us."

"When's it going to be all uncoded?"

"Well I'm trying, but you keep interrupting me."

"Cause I'm tired of watching that man nail boards."

"Spy on the ducks then," I suggested.

"I am. They never do anything secret though."

Tilley and I gave up spying for the day. We rustled out of the snowball bush, and waded upstream to visit Oscar.

Progress on the fence continued for the next couple of days. I tried not to let it bug me, but it did. The fence gave the Manor a new look of fairy-tale evil. Every time I glanced at it, my mind was taken over by the memory of Great-great-aunt Lydia's expressionless, dried-apple face. The fence made me feel different about myself. I did not feel lovable-at-first-sight anymore. When I was crossing the stream or riding across the meadow or sitting up in one of the cherry trees, I could feel Great-great-aunt Lydia's dislike touching every surface of my skin. Great-

great-aunt Lydia hated us, without even knowing us.

It bothered me to think that someone could hate me without even knowing me. It was a scary idea, especially when I was going to be starting a new school in less than two weeks. It was already the second half of August, and the reddening maples brought waves of back-to-school dread. So did the early darkness at our campfires. But what really got me in the pit of my stomach was the day-old newspaper I used to wrap up our garbage. *BACK TO SCHOOL*, threatened a full-page ad. *GET READY NOW!*

I tried to slow down the summer. If I paid five times as much attention to every moment, I reasoned, the rest of August might seem five times as long. All attention, I'd sit by the edge of the stream, studying the electric-blue dragonflies hovering like helicopters, and the spidery striders walking on water. I might have managed to slow time a bit, but I couldn't stop it.

One midnight August turned into September. A few nights later Dad doused our campfire early. "After all," he said, as the logs hissed out steam, "it's a school night."

Summer was over, long before I was ready.

NOTEBOOK: #9

NAME: Rosamund McGrady

SUBJECT: Enemy Territory

I woke up to a pink sunrise in the open porthole by my pillow. The backlit oak leaves were jewel green. The birds, who would slack off later in the day, were still singing their sunrise songs. I had a moment of perfect peace. Then I remembered. It was my first day at Windward Middle School.

I pulled back my curtain. "Your Mom and I are off," Dad said, drinking his coffee dregs.

"Already?" I asked.

"Yeah, we've got to be at the university early to straighten out our timetables," Dad said.

"Okay, then."

"Okay. So good luck on your first day," said Mom, turning in the arched doorway to blow a kiss to the top bunk.

"Yup," I said.

Something in my voice made Mom step back inside the treehouse. "You're nervous," she said.

I shrugged where I lay. Upbeat mothers don't understand nerves.

"Oh, Rosie, it will be fine. Just be yourself. And be friendly. And just join in. That's all there is to it. Really." Mom climbed a few rungs of the bunk ladder to plant an actual kiss on top of my head. "Really."

I nodded, and Mom and Dad descended through the trap door. I sat up in my bunk to get dressed for school. I had few choices for a back-to-school outfit. It was shorts weather and I had two pairs. The cargos were my favourite, and because they were my favourite I'd worn them every day. They were, when I stopped to examine them, a little grubby. My plaid shorts, on the other hand, were perfectly clean, but only because they were too ugly to wear. I wriggled into my cargos. I removed a clean T-shirt from my overstuffed drawer. It was crumpled and there was no way to press it. Since we had no electricity, we had no iron, and we had no room for an ironing board anyway.

I stood combing my hair before the locker mirror on the wall. When I combed out a twig and several pieces of bark, I started wishing I'd gone for a back-to-school hair-washing at the community centre. Too late now, I thought, peering at myself. The locker mirror was too small for me to behold my entire head at once, so I took it from its hook and moved it around to check out different portions. No individual portion looked too bad.

There was no water in our porcelain washing-up pitcher or washbasin, so I pumped some. The stream had cooled off a lot in the last weeks of August, and the water was cold on my face. I washed quickly, focussing on visible dirt. I brushed my teeth and spat over the porch banister.

Inside the treehouse, I made the lunches: a banana and jam sandwich for Tilley, and a smoked-oyster sandwich for me. I woke Tilley up for breakfast. Time proceeded. At quarter to eight, Tilley and I got our bikes from the shed and bumped across the meadow. Tilley was now riding without training wheels, and she could even ride the plank bridge across the stream. The only thing she needed me to do was push her bike up the plywood ramp to the top of Great-great-aunt Lydia's stone wall. Tilley coasted down, and together we rode the long path to the world of sidewalks and streets.

Tilley was starting Grade One at Sir Combover Elementary. I brought her to her classroom and left when she showed no signs of freaking out. Back on my bike, I continued past all the big fancy houses toward Windward Middle School. In my head I renewed the wish I'd made when my birthday candles had disappeared around the bend of the stream. The wish had been that the people at Windward would be nice.

I reached the big brick schoolhouse and locked my bike to the stand. Watching the Windward kids arrive, I couldn't tell if they were nice. All I could tell is that they definitely did not live in treehouses. I watched them getting out of Mercedes and BMWs and Range Rovers. They were well-groomed in the way of those who have hot and cold running water and full-sized mirrors. Over the summer, I had somehow forgotten that this kind of grooming was not only possible but normal. Expected even. These kids were well dressed too. Amazingly so. Every single article of clothing I saw looked like it had been bought at full price within the previous twenty-four hours by a personal shopper carrying out a wardrobe plan. In a flash of contrast, I realized that I was a mess.

I went inside to look for my classroom. The class lists were posted on the bulletin board outside the office. A bunch of kids stood around reading them. "Hey Devo, we're in the same class, man," one guy said, punching the shoulder of another guy. I guessed that Devo was *RADCLIFFE, Devon*. *MCGRADY, Rosamund*, was on the same class list.

"Rankle's class two years in a row," Devo rolled his eyes. "That really burns." For a while I watched all the boys talking to this Devo. He barely said anything and he didn't even look at them, but somehow he got their attention. Devo moved off down the hall and the other guys all moved with him, just like the fish in our stream. I followed them to my classroom and took a seat.

Other kids drifted in and sat down. When the afterclang of the nine o'clock bell was still in the air, Miss Rankle came in. She got all of us to say our names, and then she introduced herself. "My name is Miss *Rankle*," she said, as if daring us to say that it wasn't true. She was writing her name in block letters on the blackboard when the classroom door twirled open and a blonde girl twirled in. When Miss Rankle turned to glare, a bunch of other girls waved at the blonde and mouthed 'Hi'. A couple of them moved books and stuff from the seat they had been saving for her.

"You are late, Kendra," Miss Rankle said.

"Sorreeeeeeee!"

Miss Rankle started the morning with a lecture on social responsibility. I didn't really listen to her advice on how not to be a racist and how not to be a vandal. I was watching the jerking hands of the overhead clock bringing me toward my own future. The recess bell rang, sounding a bit hysterical. I pulled myself upright and went to the classroom door.

A bunch of girls were walking downstairs with the late, blonde Kendra. I tailed them. Outside they walked really slowly. Sometimes they stopped altogether, to concentrate on exclaiming or laughing. I caught up to them before I was really ready. I stood almost as close to these girls as they stood to each other. It felt weird to just attach myself to their personal space as if they were a washroom lineup or something. But wasn't that what I had to do? It was time to just join in.

"So, Kendra, was it just, like, too fun for words?" A girl named Sienna was saying this.

"I wish," said Kendra. "I just wish acting was, like, one-sixteenth as glamorous as everybody thinks. You have *no* idea. My first day on the set, I'm thinking—this is *brutal*! Like, no wonder they have to pay actresses mega millions."

"How's it so brutal?" asked another girl called Twyla.

"Where do I start? Okay, makeup," Kendra said. "I'm trapped in this chair with people swarming all over me, like, so serious you'd figure they're doing brain surgery, and every time I blink they're like—*Don't move!* And I'm like—*Okay . . . will it be all right if I keep breathing?* Then after about five hours this makeup guy calls the director over and he's like—*Oh my God! That hair! It's celestial!* He actually used that word—celestial. Weird huh? And I'm like—*It's my hair, okay, what's the big deal?*"

"Wow, you were in a movie?" I asked. I know I said it out loud, but no one else seemed to hear.

"And then we start shooting," Kendra continued, "and it's like—*More stress on the 'and'! Slower on the 'if'!* And blah blah blah blah blah. I mean, the money is great and all, but fun? Uh, no."

"How much did you get paid?" Twyla asked.

"Mom forbids me to discuss it," Kendra said. "She says it's rude to make people jealous. Anyway, she snatched my entire paycheque and stuck it in this fund thingy that I can't touch 'til I'm nineteen. And I'm like—*Mom, just let me have a thousand to spend now. Just one thousand*. And she's like—*No way! It's invested in a mutual fund, leave it alone and you'll be a wealthy woman someday.*"

"Wow," said a girl named Nova. "I'd love to be in a movie."

"Trust me, you wouldn't," Kendra said.

"What's it called again?" Twyla asked.

"*Clean Getaway*," Kendra replied.

"Let's all go see it," said Nova.

"It might not get released here," Kendra said. "Some copyright suing thingy."

"*Clean Getaway*," Twyla announced. "Starring Kendra Amelie Madeleine Smith!"

"Hardly," Kendra said. "I'm barely a co-star. Like, I'm way down there in the credits."

"Wow," I said. "How did you get the part?" To make sure I was heard this time, I had raised my voice. More than I meant to. You could say that I shouted.

"Pardon?" said Kendra. Pardon sounds like a polite thing to say, but it was not. She looked surprised and disgusted, as if I'd just tossed her a leaking lunch bag or something.

"I said, wow, how did you get the part?"

"*How did I get the part.* No offence," said Kendra, "but why are you talking to me?"

Why *was* I talking to her? Why would *anybody* talk to her? That is what I was tempted to say, but it was too risky for day one at a brand new school. Instead, I clenched my face into a smile. The smile hurt.

Sienna looked at Kendra, then at me. "Yeah," Sienna said. "Why are you, like, following us around?"

"Just . . . " I said. "Just." Still smiling, I turned away.

"This is her," Kendra whispered behind me. She was probably imitating my stupid, phony smile, but I didn't turn around to see.

My face was hot as I walked away, but I was determined to have a better joining-in experience immediately, as an urgent antidote. A game of Capture the Flag was happening on the hill that sloped down from the school toward the basketball court. The hill was the perfect place for Capture the Flag. It was all landscaped with a million beautiful shrubs, so there were lots of good ambush spots, and lots of places to hide flags. I watched as kids ran between bushes, and ran around bushes, and got tagged, and sat on the ground in invisible jail. Then a guy came streaking out of the rhododendrons, a black hoodie flapping in his hand. He was being chased, but the chaser couldn't catch him. The first guy ran and ran, then stopped and made victory arms. It was Devo. He had captured the flag, and the game was over.

As they headed to the bottom of the hill to start another game, I followed, prepared to join in. I intended to ask somebody about it. "Can I play," I would say, but no—that sounded childish. "Can I join you?" would make me sound about forty-five years old. "What team should I be on," sounded better. I was still examining this phrase for flaws, though, when everybody started running. The game was on. I was about to miss my chance. Should I just pick a team myself? Mom's voice played in my mind, telling me to just join in. Her voice was sympathetic, but a bit impatient too. So I did just join in. I ran with Devo's team into enemy territory.

I ran for all I was worth between and around and in and out of bushes. I sort of wanted to get tagged, because I thought I might meet kids in jail. Jail could be a bonding experience. No one tagged me though, so I kept on running. And then I saw the black hoodie, lying in the dust under a bright red bush. The enemy flag. It was a cool hoodie with a heart and crossbone logo and it looked more expensive than any piece of clothing I owned. I bent down and snatched it by the cuff. I had captured the flag: this would be even better than jail for my social advancement.

I turned to start my run back to home territory. Devo stood in front of me. Why was he doing that? I was on his team. He was going to wreck my victory. He was going to get me tagged. Because suddenly there were kids all around. I stepped to the left. Devo blocked my way. Then he just stared. He stared, deciding what he wanted to do with me. "Excuse me," he said, pointing to the black hoodie, "but we need that for our game." He said this very politely. He said it *too* politely, as if he was making fun of the whole idea of politeness. And what was he suggesting? That I was *stealing* the hoodie?

The game seemed to have stopped. Everybody was just standing around us watching. I held out the hoodie. A slow second later, Devo lifted his hand to take it. I knew I should just say that I wanted to join the game. But I could not say it. I turned and walked up the hill. Holding the black hoodie, Devo headed down the hill and everyone else came straggling from the bushes after him. One of the girls trailed the yellow sweatshirt that was Devo's team flag. "Okay," Devo yelled. "Let's try this again."

I'd had all the joining in that I could stand. I wanted to be alone. Not that I hadn't been alone when I was trying to talk to Kendra. Not that I hadn't been alone when I was trying to play Capture the Flag. But I wanted to be alone in private. I went to the washroom and sat in a stall, reading the manufacturer's directions for dispensing toilet paper. I left the stall and went to the sink, looking in the mirror at the face that no one, it turned out, loved at first sight. I washed my hands for something to do. In only four more minutes, recess would be over. I was making a tower of lather in the palm of my hand when another girl came into the empty washroom and stood at the sink next to me.

She brushed her hair in the mirror. "Hi!" she said brightly.

"Hi," I said, amazed to have found a friendly person.

"How are you *doing*," the girl asked, and from the warmth in her voice, I could tell that she really cared.

"Pretty good," I said. "Well, sort of nervous, actually. It's my first day at this school, and I don't know anybody, and you're actually the very first person—"

"Hold on," the girl said. "I can't hear you. I'm in a

washroom and there's someone talking right beside me. Just a sec, okay Natalie?"

The girl turned toward me, and that's when I saw the cell phone mouthpiece curved around her cheek. Her warmth had been for someone else. She had not been talking to me at all. "Were you talking to me?" she asked.

"Nope," I said. "Just talking to myself again." I faked another smile.

| | |
|---|---|
| NOTEBOOK: | #10 |
| NAME: | Rosamund McGrady |
| SUBJECT: | Breaking and Entering |

My first afternoon at Windward, I counted up all the instructional days in the school year. One hundred and ninety. One hundred and eighty-nine to go, I told myself after the first day. One hundred and eighty-eight to go. One hundred and eighty-seven.

It was hard to leave the treehouse in the mornings. Before school I'd eat my breakfast out on our porch, in the gauzy sunlight that slanted through the oak tree. I'd breathe in the special September damp earth smell. I'd inspect the perfectly perfect spider webs in the branches, sagging with jewels of dew. I was homesick for the treehouse before I'd even left it. When it was time to go to school my spirits dropped like backpacks in a dumbwaiter.

Miss Rankle was a crabby teacher, but class time wasn't what bothered me. Recess and lunch were what I hated. What made them really bad is that they were supposed to be fun. Things that are supposed to be fun and are not are a lot worse than things that are well known to be awful. When things are supposed to be fun, you feel like a big loser for not enjoying them. I spent my recesses and lunches sitting outside against the brick wall, reading about cryptography. I'd stopped trying to join in, so no one bothered being mean. My classmates left me completely alone.

Tilley could be a pain sometimes, just like every little sister. But at the end of each school day, I was always glad to see her waiting for me in front of Sir Combover with her little pink trail bike and her dinosaur helmet. I was glad to ride through the woods away from the world of school. When we got to the ramp I'd pedal so hard that my bike became airborne. My spirits would lift along with my bike. As I coasted down the ramp into the grounds of Grand Oak Manor, I felt that I was back in my own little world.

There was only one thing that stopped me from feeling truly at home on the grounds, and that was Great-great-aunt Lydia's new fence. The fence was complete by then, and delivering its unfriendly messages constantly. *Keep Out. Trespassers Will Be Prosecuted. Private Property. Beware. Guard Dog on Duty. Warning.* It was insulting, that fence. One September day as we rode our bikes across the plank bridge, we saw a new sign. It showed a stick person being thrown backward by a lightning bolt.

"Hey, a new sign," Tilley said, catching up to me on the meadow side of the stream. "What does it say?"

"Danger: Electric Fence," I read. "Now that I do not believe. That fence is so not electric."

"It might be."

"It isn't."

"How do you know?"

"It's wood, for one thing, and wood isn't a conductor. I'll show you." I veered off toward the fence.

"Rosie, don't," Tilley cried as I reached it. "I don't want you to be like that stick man!"

"I won't be. See?" I leaned from my bike and laid my hand flat against the fence. "Not electric. This fence is lying to us."

"Like the guard dog's a lie too, right?"

"Probably." A gate in the fence left a crack the width of the hinges. I got off my bike to peer for guard dogs. When I put my eye to the crack, all I could see was a narrow vertical stripe of the Manor garden, and the Manor itself beyond. "No guard dog that I can see." I rattled the gate but, just as I expected, it was locked on the inside. Tilley and I walked around the fence looking for other cracks and open knotholes. "That carpenter guy did a bad job," Tilley said. "Look, he didn't hammer the nails right." It was true. There was one place in the fence where nails stuck out two whole inches. Tilley and I wiggled them with our fingers until they were practically falling out. I managed to pull one out completely. "So," I said, dropping the nail into Tilley's hand. "Great-great-aunt Lydia's fence isn't as great as she thinks it is." We got back on our bikes and rode across the meadow to the treehouse.

Two afternoons later, Tilley and I were sitting on the treehouse porch eating honey sandwiches. Tilley was a mess of honey drips. She stood up and started for the washbasin, but stopped suddenly. "Rosie," she said. "It's that car!"

I jumped up beside her. Through the screen of oak

leaves I glimpsed Great-great-aunt Lydia's Bentley driving slowly out the stable door. At the speed of a parade float it bumped along the drive to the curly iron gates in the stone wall that separated the grounds from Bellemonde Drive. The curly iron gates magically opened for the Bentley. Or, it looked magical, but obviously Great-great-aunt Lydia had had them retrofitted with automatic openers. The Bentley paused while the gates opened, then disappeared onto Bellemonde Drive.

"Great-great-aunt Lydia's gone." I turned toward Tilley. "The Manor's empty. We can explore."

I hurried down to the shed, grabbed our hammer and rode my bike across the meadow. Stopping at the loose board, I began prying out nails. It was what Miss Rankle would call ironic. Before there was a fence to keep us out, I'd never considered trespassing into Great-great-aunt Lydia's garden, but the fence had somehow dared me to get inside. I left just one nail to hold the board in place. I swung the board on the single nail and a gap opened in the fence. I stuck my head inside.

"It's big enough," I said. "Good."

"Maybe we shouldn't go in," said Tilley, who had caught up to me.

"Why not?"

"Great-great-aunt Lydia will do that thing to us. The thing she does to trespassers."

"Prosecute us? No she won't. That's just another lie, like the electric fence and the guard dog." I put one foot over the hedge, swiveled my hips sideways, and followed with my other foot. I was inside. It was weird. Before the fence had been built I'd stood about a foot away from where I was now standing, looking right at this very spot. But this familiar spot felt thrillingly different, now that I was inside. I was violating Great-great-aunt Lydia's space.

"Come on Tilley," I said, all bad influence. Tilley slipped through the fence behind me, and we stood looking at the paths that wound through the garden. There were half a dozen to choose from.

"Pick a path," I said, and we began to explore. The path was soft and mossy, but somehow our footsteps sounded exaggerated, like what a rabbit must hear. We wound our way between shrubs and came to a little fountain. Water spouted from the mouth of a man's stone face, into a stone basin. It did not seem pleasant, for something to gush so forcefully from a person's mouth. We continued down the forking paths.

We came to a pond, which we'd never seen properly from outside the hedge. The pond water was as dark as anti-matter. At first it seemed empty, but then enormous golden carp rose from the depths. They watched Tilley and me from the surface, and opened their gaping mouths as if getting ready to swallow us whole. They were prehistorically huge.

"These fish are man-eaters," I told Tilley.

"Are not," she said.

"Are too." I threw in a chunk of leftover granola bar, and from the way those fish thrashed, it seemed that it might be true.

"Let's go, Rosie," Tilley said, pulling on the cuff of my fleece jacket.

"Okay," I said, because it was hard not to be creeped-out by those fish. We followed another path to a tree that had been all perfectly trimmed into the shape of a deer, with antlers and everything.

"This used to be a real deer," I said.

"Did not," Tilley said.

"Did too. It was a real deer, until Great-great-aunt Lydia put an evil spell on it."

"She did not."

"She did!" I thought of something, and got the torn blue strip out of my wallet. "'Ives. It Turns. Possessed A. Treehouse I. It Turns O. You Are Who. It Turns Ou.'" I quoted. "You know what this is about Tilley? It's about a spell, where you *turn* three times. It's about the spell that made the deer *possessed*."

"That is so not true. I saw the gardener clipping it."

"It *is* true," I said. I didn't believe what I was saying, but this dark view of Great-great-aunt Lydia suited my mood.

"Then why does it say 'treehouse', and 'you are who'," challenged Tilley.

"It's saying we in the treehouse are next." I took the coded letter out of my wallet and waved it. "And *this* isn't a code at all. It's the words of the spell. If someone chants this while circling a creature three times, the creature turns into something else. For all eternity."

"Does not."

"It does!" I began to circle Tilley, reading from the coded letter in a creepy voice. "ID ID NO! TE VERTHIN KAPA! IROFSCIS! SORSCO!"

"Rosie!" Tilley smiled a bit to show that she knew I was teasing.

"ULDDO SOMU! CHHARM IHA! VETOLE AVETH!"

"Rosie, stop it!"

"ISBLO!" I cried, circling. "ODYHO!"

"Don't!" Tilley screamed, and she ran for the gap in the fence, leaving me alone in the Manor garden. I looked around. Up in one of Great-great-aunt Lydia's trees was an owl. His head turned weirdly, almost a complete turn, as if it was a jar lid or something. The owl glared. I decided not to explore any further. There was no way of knowing when Great-great-aunt Lydia might return in her Bentley.

"You're *mean*," Tilley said as I crouched through the gap in the fence.

"You knew I was teasing," I said, swinging the board shut behind me.

"You scared me on purpose."

"You were scared of being turned into a *tree*? And you're the child of *scientists*?"

Tilley's eyeballs got wet and shiny. "You're *really* mean," she said. As she marched across the meadow, I felt a bit bad. I *had* known she was scared, and as an older sibling I had a responsibility not to abuse my power. I followed her to the treehouse and made her hot chocolate on the camping stove, and read her a chapter of Harry Potter, and she went right back to being happy with me.

The next day after school I noticed that Great-great-aunt Lydia's fence didn't bug me anymore. I figured it was because we had committed the breaking and entering. The fence insulted us, but we had insulted it right back.

That Thursday afternoon when I arrived at Sir Combover Elementary, Tilley was holding hands with a cute little blonde girl. "I'm invited to Eveline's," Tilley announced.

"I don't know if you're allowed," I said.

"Phone and ask." Tilley pointed to the cell phone that I borrowed from Dad on school days. I flipped it open and called Mom at the university. Of course Tilley could go to Eveline's, Mom said; she and Dad would pick her up on their way home.

"You can go," I reported and they hopped around all happy. I got back on my bike and rode home alone.

Tilley started going to Eveline's almost every day after school. It felt weird to be at the treehouse by myself. After being by myself at school all day, I didn't like it much. Sometimes I did my homework. Sometimes I worked on decoding Great-great-aunt Lydia's letter. I tried all the words from the torn blue strip as key words. I wrote out one possible alphabet after another, starting them with 'turns' and 'forgive' and 'bones' and 'ground' and 'someday'. Sometimes, when I sat alone with my pen and paper, the great volume of silence and stillness and time was too much. Then I'd practice bicycle jumps off the ramp over Great-great-aunt Lydia's stone wall. Or I'd go jump onto the rope swing and my feelings would rush out of my body. Then, when I was tired of everything else, I'd just sit on the porch and watch the oak leaves spiral down to the meadow until Mom and Dad and Tilley finally came home.

At our nightly campfires, Mom asked motherly questions.

"So how was school today?"

"Good."

"Yeah? Good? So tell me about your classmates, what are they like?"

"They're like kids in Grade Seven."

"And you're getting to know some of them?"

"I see them every day, yeah."

"So tell me about some of them. Who are the friendly ones?"

"Everybody is of equal friendliness. Do we have to keep having this conversation? Haven't we already had it, like, eleven times?"

"Don't get snippy, Rosie, your mother's just interested," Dad said.

"Okay," I sighed.

I had succeeded in ending the conversation. Mom closed up the bag of marshmallows and stoked the fire. I sat on my stump in silence, watching the sparks as they rose and twisted and mingled with the stars.

NOTEBOOK: #11

NAME: Rosamund McGrady

SUBJECT: Valuable Lesson

It was in the third week of September that I had my first real encounter with Bridget Hanrahan. She sat across the aisle from me. We'd spoken exactly three times.

Time #1:
Bridget: I HATE mechanical pencils! These stupid feeble leads! Do you have a pencil I could borrow?
Me: I think so. Yup. Here.

Time #2:
Bridget: (indicating back of T-shirt). Your tag is sticking out.
Me: (tucking tag back in). Oh, okay, thanks.

Time #3:
Bridget: What's our math homework? Do you know?
Me: Chapter Seven, page 79, section B, questions 13 to 29.
Bridget: Brutal. Thanks.

This made her slightly friendlier than the other kids in my class, but even so my opinion of Bridget was low. She was good friends with Kendra. This did not reflect well on Bridget.

Our encounter happened in communication skills, the last class of the day. I was dying of boredom. Miss Rankle was lecturing on transitive versus intransitive verbs. I knew there would be a test on this stuff, but I knew it would be a multiple-choice-pick-the-correct-sentence test. Not to brag or anything, but I speak excellent English, and I trusted myself to pick the correct sentence without listening to one single word that Miss Rankle said. I got my wallet out of my cargo pants. I took out Great-great-aunt Lydia's coded letter and lay it on my desk. I tried to think of new ways to write a code alphabet, and started writing one where I switched every second letter.

BADCFEHG, I wrote. I glanced up to see Bridget Hanrahan looking across the aisle at my desk top. She nodded at the coded letter and my partial alphabet. With a quizzical smile she traced a question mark in the air. It had actually been awhile since anyone outside my family had smiled at me. It had been awhile since anyone outside my family had shown any interest in me. That is why I did what I did. I smiled back, and I passed Great-great-aunt Lydia's coded letter to Bridget.

"An *intransitive* verb is an action verb that does *not* require an object to *complete its action*," Miss Rankle said, from the front of the class. "A *transitive* verb is one that expresses an action *directed* toward a *person*, or a *thing*." Miss Rankle spoke without any pause or change of tone, so Bridget and I didn't notice her heading down the aisle until it was too late. Bridget glanced up at Miss Rankle's looming pantsuit and closed the coded letter in her hand. Miss Rankle grabbed Bridget's wrist. "For example, the *teacher demanded* the note," Miss Rankle said, actually prying Bridget's fingers open. Miss Rankle seized Great-great-aunt Lydia's coded letter.

"Passing *notes*," Miss Rankle said. "That's something I haven't seen in a while. I thought it had gone out of style since text messaging. But apparently not," Miss Rankle said. She smoothed Great-great-aunt Lydia's letter. "And in code, too. Intriguing. I'm sure the class will be fascinated to hear what it says. Do tell, Rosamund, since it appears from the stationery that you're the author."

"I'm not, actually," I said. "I don't know what it says."

Miss Rankle looked at me. I could hear the air leaving her nostrils. "Not the author, even though your surname is right at the top of the stationery? I find that hard to believe. Very hard. I find it easier to believe that you are choosing to be difficult. But you should know, Rosamund, that I can also choose to be difficult."

I knew that already. I had heard lots of kids in the class say so. When she chose to be difficult, she gave out test scores that were actually in the negative, wiping out earlier good grades. When she chose to be difficult, she gave long detentions for offences like pencil-dropping. When she chose to be difficult, she made kids sing solos in Music class. I stared at the floor to avoid her threatening stare. If Miss Rankle chose to be difficult, my Grade Seven year would be terrible. So should I pretend that I had lied at first, and pretend that I *did* know what the note said? What would I say about what the note said? I tried to think of possible note topics, but my imagination failed. My mind contained nothing at all, except what was right before my eyes. I was about to say that the note was about squares of grey linoleum with a random pattern of pink and black spots when Bridget spoke up.

"Rosie's mother Lydia wrote the note," Bridget said. "Both our mothers had to write in code for Pathfinders. Rosie and I are trying to earn our Pathfinders' cryptography badge. We have to decode encrypted messages using the same steganography principles developed by Trimethius. You know, like the Nazis used for the World War II Enigma machine? And like the US Navy used to develop the Cryptanalytic Bombe to break the Nazi's code? It's really, really hard though. That's why our leader said that the code has to be written by somebody we know well. To give us a clue. Otherwise it would be impossible. And we're really, really sorry we passed the note in class, but we've been working really, really hard to decode it, and we're just so intellectually stimulated by the challenge."

I stared at Bridget, totally impressed. Miss Rankle stared at Bridget too, assessing her credibility. "Well, Bridget and Rosamund, I'm sorry that all your hard work is going to end up going to *waste*. No doubt that will help you learn the valuable lesson that there is a time and a place for everything." With that Miss Rankle walked away and shut Great-great-aunt Lydia's coded letter into her top desk drawer. She turned the key to lock it. I stared at the tasseled key, feeling gutted. Great-great-aunt Lydia's coded letter, gone!

"*Now*. Back to more *important* matters. Transitive verbs fall into *two categories*," Miss Rankle's voice vibrated. "We call these *active* and *passive voice*."

Bridget raised her hand.

"Yes Bridget?"

"May I please go to the water fountain?"

"To the water fountain? Oh, very well," Miss Rankle said, sounding all annoyed, which goes to show just how little it takes with her. Bridget rose from her seat and headed past Miss Rankle toward the door. "Then there are verb *moods*, which are not to be confused with verb *voices*." Miss Rankle said. "Verb *moods* are of three kinds: *indicative*, *imperative* and *subjunctive*." As Miss Rankle looked critically from student to student, Bridget hesitated in the threshold of the open classroom door. When Miss Rankle went on about verb moods, Bridget came back inside the classroom to Miss Rankle's desk. Bridget turned the tasseled key. Slowly, she slid the top drawer open. Miss Rankle made eye contact with me and I nodded as if begging to know more about the subjunctive mood. Bridget removed Great-great-aunt Lydia's coded letter and slowly shut the drawer. Letter in hand, she left the classroom. But in seconds she was back with the letter. She had lost her nerve, I thought, and I couldn't blame her. Stealing the coded letter was suicide: Miss Rankle would have known for sure that Bridget was the thief. Of course she had to put it back. The opening drawer caught Miss Rankle's ear.

"Bad grammar!" I yelled. I did this to create a distraction. I didn't have a lot of time to think, but I knew that bad grammar was Miss Rankle's obsession. And Miss

Rankle *was* distracted. She was totally examining me. Behind her back Bridget shut the coded letter away in the drawer and turned the tasseled key. I was struck again by its loss and that was all I could think of for a moment. But Miss Rankle was waiting for me to finish my sentence. "Bad grammar . . ." I repeated. "Bad grammar . . . it's . . . it's said by some to signal the end of civilization. Do you think that's true?"

I sounded like the biggest nerd ever, but I had a moral obligation to protect Bridget. She'd attempted a serious offence on my behalf.

"That is a rather profound thought, Rosamund," Miss Rankle said, and she actually looked a tiny bit pleased. "And yes, I do think it's true."

Bridget returned to her seat and started writing. When Miss Rankle was chalking verb tenses on the board, Bridget leaned over and stuck a scrap of paper inside my desk. I unfolded it.

I TOOK PIX OF YOUR NOTE WITH MY PHONE.

I breathed. Great-great-aunt Lydia's actual letter was gone for good, but the code had been saved. I flipped the scrap over and wrote THANKS, YOU SAVED MY LIFE. This was a bit of an exaggeration, but I have always considered it good manners to exaggerate when thanking somebody. To stress my gratitude, I added five exclamation marks. I crumpled the scrap, leaned over and tossed it into Bridget's desk.

Bridget uncrumpled it and smiled at me. I'd never really looked at her face before. It was a nice face. There was a space between her front teeth. Her eyes were the same colour as the pebble-bottom of our stream. She had freckles: not a big mass of them, but just a few really clear ones, like dot-to-dots. Even though she was friends with Kendra, I thought Bridget had the face of someone I'd like to know.

NOTEBOOK: #12

NAME: Rosamund McGrady

SUBJECT: The Lunch Exchange

The following morning when the recess bell rang, Bridget reached into her desk.

"Here," she said, as we stood in our aisles. "These are the pictures I took of your note. I took six, but only two turned out."

"Thank you so much," I said. "So, so, so much. I wanted to say thanks yesterday, but you disappeared as soon as the bell rang."

"Bridget! Are you *coming*?" Kendra called from the classroom door.

"In a minute," Bridget called back. Kendra did not look pleased.

"That was completely amazing," I said to Bridget, "the way you stole it right out of Miss Rankle's desk. Weren't you scared?"

"Yeah, but what choice did I have? Since she didn't believe me about our cryptography badge."

"Oh, I think she believed you. She just felt like being mean. It was brilliant, your story about our cryptography badge. I was, like—how is she coming up with all this stuff? About Trimethius and the Enigma Machine and the . . . stegasaurography? No. Stega-whatever."

"Steganography." Bridget shrugged. "Believe it or not, that's what my dad talks about at the dinner table. He's really into military history. Anyway, glad you were impressed."

"I was in awe. That was so nice of you, too, to go to all that trouble to defend my note."

"Bridget," Kendra called. "You're wasting our whole recess. Let's *go*."

"You go," Bridget called back. "I'll catch up with you."

She turned from Kendra to me. "It would have really bugged me to lose your note. I thought it might be important. What's the story anyway? Do you really not know what it says?"

"No, I really don't."

"So who wrote it? That Lydia Florence Augustine person?"

"Yup."

"Is she a relative?"

"Yeah, she's my Great-great-aunt, except that I've never met her, cause there was some huge fight in my family decades before I was even born."

"So how did you get the note?"

I was not quite ready, in my very first conversation with Bridget, to say that I'd found it in the treehouse where I lived. "I found it at my place," I said, "when we moved in this summer."

"So the letter must be old, then," Bridget said, "Because this Lydia person wouldn't have been at your place after the big family breakup, would she?"

This was not necessarily true, seeing that my place was an unlocked treehouse on Great-great-aunt Lydia's own property. I shrugged.

"Plus it seems like kind of an olden-days thing, to write in code, don't you think?" Bridget continued. "'Cause they didn't have cell phones or BlackBerries or whatever back then. Not even private land lines. So they had to be more creative to communicate secretly."

"Yeah, I guess."

"What was the big family fight all about?"

"No clue. Everybody involved in the fight is dead now, except for Great-great-aunt Lydia."

"Maybe her note explains it."

"That's what I'm hoping."

"Bridget!" Kendra was still waiting. "Come! On!"

"Cool. Well, good luck with it," Bridget said, as she headed to the front of the classroom to join Kendra. Kendra pivoted in the doorway, swirling her hair like a satin cape.

After recess came math. Whenever I looked up from my text, Kendra was staring at me from her eye-corners like one of those paintings whose eyes follow you all around the room. When the lunch bell rang, Bridget came up to me. "Want to have lunch?"

"Yeah, okay," I said getting my lunch bag. "Sure."

"Rosie's going to have lunch with us," Bridget reported to Kendra.

Kendra sighed through her nostrils. "What*ever*," she said.

She walked down the hallway with Sienna, Twyla and Nova. Bridget and I followed a couple of steps behind. We headed outside to a picnic table in the courtyard. I knew from eavesdropping that this area was called the Lunch Exchange. Nova and Twyla sat on one side of the table, then slid over to make room for Bridget. She sat beside them. Kendra and Sienna sat on the other side of the table. They did not slide over to make room for me. I stood holding my lunch bag.

"Come on you guys," Bridget directed. "Shove over for Rosie."

Sienna and Kendra looked me over head to toe and shuffled their butts two and a half inches to the left. As I sat down, they watched me as though they were grading my performance. I didn't want to sit too close. I sat with half my butt on the bench, the other half off.

Bridget put her zip-locked sandwich in centrepiece position on the picnic table. "Chicken salad," she announced. "Which I am so totally not in the mood for."

"You're not in the mood for chicken salad?" Twyla asked. "Are you insane?"

"Depends who you ask," Bridget said.

"Trade you for peanut butter and honey then," said Twyla.

"But chicken's worth more."

"Uh-uh. Peanut butter's illegal. That makes it valuable," said Twyla.

"Does not. The Supervee could confiscate it."

"Then how about, I'll give you the rest of these." Twyla looked inside her bag of barbecue potato chips. "Five eighths of a bag. Maybe eleven sixteenths. You must act now to receive this generous offer."

"Deal." Bridget turned to me. "What sandwich do you have?"

"Smoked oyster," I said.

"Never heard of that," Bridget said. "Are they hard to trade?"

"Never tried. I love smoked oyster."

"Have some chips," Bridget said, and I took one.

Kendra burst the air with a laugh. "Remember at summer camp," she said. "That peanut butter? And that tire?" They all laughed, Bridget too. "And the flying spoon?"

"Spoons and Ammo!" Sienna declared, and they all killed themselves laughing.

"And Counselor Bob when she caught us?" Kendra said.

"The call of the pileated woodpecker!" Everyone shouted it out, but laughter wrecked their timing.

I forced a smile. "What's the story?" I asked.

"Oh, you wouldn't think it was funny," said Kendra.

"No," Sienna said. "You wouldn't get it."

"No," Twyla agreed. "You had to be there."

"Then let's talk about something else," Bridget said. "'Cause Rosie *wasn't* there. Who's started that Ancient Egypt project?"

"Remember Counselor Bob?" Kendra continued as if Bridget hadn't spoken. "One's groundsheet must never exceed . . ."

"The perimeter of one's tent!" shrieked Kendra, Sienna, Twyla and Nova, and they were in hysterics again. Bridget and I started talking about possible Ancient Egypt projects. We were about forty-eight seconds into our conversation when Devo arrived and raised a professional looking sandwich above his head. “Okay,” he called to everybody at the Lunch Exchange. “Prosciutto and provolone on focaccia. What am I bid?”

“Tuna?” offered one guy.

“Boring,” Devo declared.

“Chicken?” asked Twyla.

“Miracle whip or mayo?” Devo asked. Twyla looked to Bridget for the answer.

“Miracle whip,” Bridget said.

“Gag. Forget it. Doesn’t anybody have anything that’s actually edible? What’s this?” Without even asking, Devo took my smoked oyster sandwich and pulled up a corner of the bread. “Oh, God! *Slugs?*”

“They’re not slugs,” said Bridget.

“You know, I’ve seen some gross things at the Lunch Exchange, but *that* is the grossest,” Devo said. “Definitely the grossest. A *slug* sandwich. That’s right out of Fear Factor.”

“They’re smoked oysters,” I said. My ears were hot.

Devo flipped off the top piece of bread and held my sandwich open-faced on his palm. “Slugs? Slugs anybody?” he said, making the rounds to all the picnic tables. “Nice fresh slug sandwich? Come on, people! Somebody bid something! Chewed gum, maybe? Some pop backwash?”

He returned to our table and brought my sandwich right up to Sienna’s face. “How about you?”

“Eeeeewwwww,” she said, leaning away. Devo rushed my sandwich at Kendra, and she actually screamed.

“How do slugs taste?” Devo asked me.

“I wouldn’t know,” I said, wishing that I was not a blusher. It is impossible to pretend that things aren’t getting to you when you are blushing severely.

"Or is it the texture you like? The little bursts of guts?"

"I think I'm going to be sick," said Kendra.

"Quite the delicacy," Devo said, dropping my sandwich back on my waxed paper. A smoked oyster fell to the ground. He stamped on it and twisted his heel.

"You're a jerk Devon," Bridget said.

He faked a gasp. "Oh! She called me a jerk! Oh! My self esteem! Get me some counseling."

"*That* would be a good idea," Bridget said.

"Mine always are," Devo said.

"So, you're *admitting* you need counseling?" Bridget asked.

Devo nodded. "To cope with the horror of seeing you."

"I'll spare us both. Come on Rosie." Bridget said, getting up from the picnic table. "Something stinks around here."

"Uh," Devo said. "That would be the slug sandwich."

Bridget walked off, dark hair swinging, back perfectly straight. She looked great. I followed after her, all hot and red, a half sandwich in each hand, and my juice bottle under my arm. Kendra and Sienna and Twyla and Nova sat watching us go.

"That guy!" Bridget said. "He is *such* a troublemaker! You know he even says making trouble is his hobby?"

"That's weird," I said.

"It's mental," Bridget agreed.

"Why does everybody like him then?"

"Everybody *doesn't* like him."

"I thought he was popular," I said.

"He is."

"Well, that means people like him, doesn't it?"

"Not really," said Bridget. "It's not exactly the same thing."

"What's the difference?"

"The difference?" Bridget thought. "Hard to explain."

"So why is he *popular* then?"

Bridget shrugged. "Looks cool, acts cool, has cool stuff."

"What cool stuff?" I wanted to know.

"Like *everything*," said Bridget. "He's really rich. You must know that already: he brags about it enough. He's got more stuff than you could even think up. His mom actually orders his recess snacks from some big-deal catering place in New York, if you can believe that. Designer junk food. He's totally spoiled."

I felt okay as long as I was with Bridget trashing Devo. Afterward, though, sitting in communication skills with no one but Miss Rankle to distract me, I was bothered again. While Miss Rankle talked about conjunctions, my worries formed a dark mass in my mind. The dark thought I had was this: if the kids at Windward gave me this much trouble about having a different sandwich, what were they going to do when they found out I lived in a treehouse?

| NOTEBOOK: | #13 |
| --- | --- |
| NAME: | Rosamund McGrady |
| SUBJECT: | Very Own Style |

It had been the nicest summer on record and the good weather continued the whole first month of school. Every night in September we ate dinner at the campfire, cooking on the metal grill over the embers. We were barbecuing chicken on the very last night of September when I felt something hit the top of my head. "It's raining," said Tilley, and suddenly it was. Rain pocked the dust around our campfire and the air was full of that rain-on-dust smell. We wrapped our half-grilled dinner in foil and put it in the dumbwaiter, along with some fire logs. As we climbed the ladder to the treehouse, the oak leaves quivered with rain. By the time we winched up our dinner and firewood, we were clinging wet. Inside the treehouse, all was in dull shadow, and the stove was cold. Mom dumped everything from the foil into a frying pan. Dad knelt down to build our first-ever fire in the cast-iron stove.

The rain fell harder. It pinged on our tin chimney out

in the oak branches, and it drummed like fingers on the treehouse roof. I had a thought. "What am I going to wear in the rain," I asked. "I've got no rain gear. Tilley either."

"That's what you think," said Mom, lighting the camping stove.

"You got us some?" I didn't get many new clothes, so I was interested.

"I did."

"So are you gonna show us?"

"If you want," said Mom, turning the heat down to low. She looked so pleased that I got all hopeful. That was dumb of me, but I'd temporarily forgotten that she was pleased by pretty much everything. She crouched at the drawer under her bunk and tugged something out.

"Ta DA!" She held up two capes. "Made them myself."

The capes were a throbbing, chemical orange. They were made of plastic. As for their style, it had clearly been inspired by Little Red Riding Hood. As the orange capes pulsated at my eyeballs, Mom bragged that she had made them from a three-dollar tarp. She'd also made gaiters to keep our legs dry, she said, displaying four weird Scrooge McDuck sort of things. Because we had no sewing machine, she said, she'd just glued everything together.

"Has it ever occurred to you that Red Riding Hood was actually *named* after her rain gear," I said.

"No," Mom said. "It hasn't."

"And if I wear this in public, I'll be Orange Plastic Hood. It will become my identity."

"I don't think so, Rosie."

Tilley was looking at the capes too. "The little one's mine, right?" she asked.

"Right," Mom said, and she twirled the cape for Tilley to admire.

Tilley took a turn at twirling the cape herself. "Cool," she said. Obviously she was completely starved for dress-up clothes. I, however, knew the cape was totally uncool, and I felt it was my sisterly duty to let her know.

"Tilley, it is so not cool," I advised. "It's hideous."

It didn't seem fair that I got such a big lecture just for trying to educate my little sister. We weren't made of money, Mom said, and did I have any idea what it cost to buy a rain jacket and pants; and our capes had industrial mildew-retardant, which was important when your only closet was a shed; and she'd spent a lot of time making them when she had important research to do; and she thought I'd appreciate it but instead I was rude and surly and ungrateful; and why was I so insecure anyway, because didn't I realize that all I had to do was believe that my cape was cool and everyone else would believe it too?

"Like the emperor's new clothes," Tilley suggested helpfully.

Mom pushed her eyebrows together. "Sort of," she said and finally the lecture came to an end.

If we lived in a bigger place Mom and I would have stomped off to different rooms, but in the treehouse on a rainy evening all I could do was stomp two steps to the left while she stomped two steps to the right. All the tension stayed highly concentrated in that small space. Mom stood at the frying pan, attacking our dinner with a wooden spoon. I set the knives and forks on our checkered tablecloth with more force than was strictly necessary. After dinner I washed the dishes in our plastic washbasin, and hurled the steaming dishwater over the porch railing. I did my homework by kerosene lamp until climbing off to bed. That whole evening I barely spoke to Mom.

In the morning the roof was pattering and my porthole streamed with dribbles. I pulled back my curtain and got out of my bunk. The wooden ladder was cold on my bare feet, and I could see my breath. Through the belly door of the cast-iron stove, I saw cold, grey ash. There was no firewood in the treehouse; it was all out on the rainy porch. My feet were turning all white and ghoulish on the treehouse floor. I would be freezing by the time I got a fire lit. I climbed back into bed, and eventually Dad got up and made the fire.

The porch firewood was rain-soaked, and Dad's fire was not a success. There was a lot of hissing and a lot of smoke, but not much flame or warmth. Mom made porridge on the camping stove and we cradled our bowls to warm our fingers. When it was time to leave for school the rain was still bouncing off the porch boards. I was already way too cold to let myself get wet. I put on my awful cape, and I even put on the bizarre gaiters. Vain choices about outerwear are for people with central heating. Tilley put on her own miniature cape.

Mom had calmed during the night. "Have a nice day girls," she said, kissing us both on the tops of our heads. My kiss crackled like thunder through my plastic hood. Although I hated to admit it to myself, our rain gear *was* very practical. The weird gaiters kept our legs dry in the wet meadow grass. The hideous capes were waterproof, but roomy enough not to be sweaty. When Tilley and I got on our bikes, they sheltered our legs but didn't interfere with pedaling. I began to feel a grudging appreciation of them as we made the long ride through the rain and the new mud.

When I arrived at Windward, Kendra was standing undercover with Sienna, Twyla and Nova. The instant I saw them, I hated my rain gear again. Waterproofness is not prized by kids who are only out in the rain between their heated SUVs and their heated schools. Fashion is. Kendra's group was not dressed for rain. As I got off my bike they all looked me over, from hood to gaiters and hood again.

"Omigosh!" Kendra said as I approached the bike rack. "That's so cute! Barbie clothes in life size!"

"Yeah, wow," Sienna said. "So orange! Quite a fashion statement."

"Yeah, Rosie definitely has her very own style," Twyla said, and the three of them exchanged mean smiles.

I went into the cloakroom and took off my rain outfit. Instead of hanging it to dry out in public view, I folded it into my backpack. I sat at my desk. As the morning bell rang, Bridget slid into her desk across the aisle. I was glad to see her. She was Windward's only friendly face.

It rained hard until after recess. Halfway through socials the rain stopped, and by the end of the class the sun beamed through the classroom windows. I felt ecstatically warm. Everybody else got hot and stripped down to T-shirts, but I kept my jacket on. I felt like heat was a precious commodity that I was storing up for cold times.

The noon bell rang. "Coming for lunch Rosie?" Bridget asked.

"Sure," I said, wishing I could hang out with just Bridget and not her nasty friends. We headed for the Lunch

Exchange. Nobody was sitting: the picnic tables were still too wet. Devo walked up to me, hands in pockets.

"Got a sec?" he asked me. Matt and Zach and Heath hung in the background.

"*What?*" I asked.

Devo sighed. "Okay. Friday? At lunch? Your sandwich? Just. . . . I felt like sort of a jerk later. For going on about it. Sorry, I guess, is what I'm saying."

"What, are the Supervees making you say this or something?" I asked. He did seem sorry though.

"Nobody *makes* me do anything. I just thought later that it might have made you feel bad. Cause you're new, and all."

I nodded once.

"So I brought you something. To eat."

I remembered Devo's designer junk food from New York. "Yeah?"

"Yeah," he nodded and he stuck out his arm. "Your favourite." His hand was so close to my face that it took a moment to refocus on the glistening thing he held. It was a big green slug, waving its feelers in slow motion. It was the most revolting thing I'd ever seen close up. As I jumped back, I heard this wimpy little scream. I am sorry to say that it was me.

Matt and Zach and Heath were yukking it up, but Devo's face hadn't changed. "Help yourself," he invited, all gracious. I didn't know how he could hold that slug in his bare hand.

"Get that away from her," Bridget demanded.

I backed away until the bricks of the school were right behind me.

"Come on, try it," Devo said, and he chucked the slug underhand. His aim was perfect. The slug belly sucked onto my forearm and held. I thought I might pass out from horror, but I didn't. I flapped my arm to get it off. Devo and Co. all found this hilarious, but the flapping had no effect on the slug. It clung to me. My brain pulsed. Should I flick it off? I'd have to touch it with my bare hand. Brush it against the building? I might squish its guts out. I flapped harder.

Bridget picked up a stick. She stepped forward with it cautiously, a bit at a time, as though she were going to tame a lion. She poked at the slug, and when she nudged it off my arm she leaped backward, as though the slug might make a lunge for her. I'm not criticizing though. I would have done exactly the same.

The slug hit the courtyard and curled up, traumatized by the poke, the fall and the grit. Devo bent to pick it up. I was not about to go through the same ordeal again. I ran.

Feet pounded behind me.

"Try it," Matt called.

"Eat it," Zach giggled stupidly, all out of breath.

I wrenched open the door of the girls' washroom and charged into sudden silence. With a paper towel I rubbed silver slime off my forearm. My knees were shaking. I was probably more traumatized than the slug. As the washroom door swung open I prepared to defend myself. But it was not my attackers. It was Bridget.

"You okay?" Her voice reverbed off the white tile walls.

"Yeah," I said.

"What a total psychopath Devo is," she said.

"Total," I agreed.

"Don't go outside," Bridget warned. "The three of them are right by the door." There was no other exit from the washroom: the door to the hallway was locked because of Windward's rule that students have to stay outside at lunch.

"Jerks," I said.

"Total jerks. Let's just stay here," Bridget said, "so they waste their whole lunch hour waiting."

"Okay." I was touched by Bridget's offer to keep me company in a smelly school washroom.

"Not much to do though, is there," Bridget said.

"No." I was worried that she'd get bored. "Ever notice your reflection in the paper towel dispenser? Lean close."

Bridget put her face near the warped silver metal. "Hey yeah," she said. "Cyclops eye."

"Go back a bit."

"Weird! Three eyes!"

We leaned from different angles, checking out our pear-shaped faces, and our hourglass faces, and our faces shaped like light bulbs. We were killing ourselves laughing when two Grade Eight girls came in. "Our turn," one declared, and they crowded us away from the dispenser.

"Okay, I thought up something else," Bridget said. "Take a paper towel and bunch it up and stand back here and aim for the spot that turns on the automatic hand dryer," she said. "We can keep score with toilet paper. One piece per point."

Before I knew it lunch hour was over. I was sorry to hear the one o'clock bell, and I think Bridget was too. We stayed a few minutes extra to break the tie. When we headed to our classroom everyone else in the class was already in the hallway waiting for the door to open. Kendra watched us approach with her eye corners. "Want to come to my place after school?" Bridget asked me. I guess Bridget thought that if we could have fun in a school washroom, we could have fun anywhere.

NOTEBOOK: #14

NAME: Rosamund McGrady

SUBJECT: The Lie

Of course I could go to Bridget's after school, Mom said when I called her at the linguistics lab. She sounded thrilled that I had made a friend. I was thrilled too. Only one thing worried me as I sat in communication skills, waiting for the 3:20 bell. If Bridget and I were going to be friends, I was going to have to tell her that I lived in a treehouse. I didn't have a problem telling Bridget, but I did not want Kendra to find out. Or Devo. Or Sienna. Or Twyla or Nova. Or Matt or Heath or Zach. Not yet, anyway. When I was more established at Windward Middle School I would come out about living in a treehouse. So when I told Bridget about the treehouse after school that day, I would ask her to keep it a secret. I trusted her to keep a secret.

Bridget's Mom, Paige, picked us up after school. She put my bike in the back of her minivan and drove us to Bridget's house. Windward is totally surrounded by fancy houses, so I shouldn't have been so freaked that one of them was Bridget's. I'd just never been inside a house like that before, and I wasn't ready for how big it was up close.

"Here we are," Paige said, idling the minivan while the automatic garage door rolled away. The garage was three times the size of the entire treehouse. From the garage we entered a room that was more treehouse sized. It was "the mud room," which was basically a giant closet for boots and umbrellas and stuff. Beyond that was the family room. It was huge. There was so much space that you could hardly stub a toe if you were trying. Our little treehouse suddenly seemed a bit pathetic.

"Snack, girls?" Paige asked, putting down a plate of homemade chocolate-chip cookies. These cookies were heaven. They were a million times better than packaged, and several zillion times better than Mom's campfire cookies. Even the Hanrahan milk was better than ours, because a propane fridge is never cold enough. I drained my glass in four glugs. Paige refilled it, then sat at the table and started asking questions. I didn't mind to begin with. Her first questions could all be answered with a simple yes. Yes, I was new to Windward. Yes, I had gone to Queen's Heights before. Yes, I liked Windward. But yes, I did miss my old friends.

Then Paige asked me a harder question. "Whereabouts do you live?"

I was already losing my nerve about explaining the treehouse to Bridget. Even less did I want to explain it to Paige, who probably had no interest in rope swings or dumbwaiters. Her own house must be what she liked, I reasoned: therefore the treehouse would sound cramped and inconvenient to her. And how could I swear Paige to secrecy, an adult I'd just met? But if she wasn't sworn, she'd tell other mothers, and pretty soon Devo and Kendra would know everything. When I told Bridget about the treehouse, we had to be alone.

"Where do I live? Um. Out that way," I answered, waving my hand around.

"On the University Endowment Lands?" Paige asked.

"Yes," I said truthfully.

"Oh, lovely. That's such a nice area. Beautiful woods. Which street do you live on?"

The conversation was not going well. I didn't live on a street at all. The treehouse was nowhere near one. And yet Paige's very question showed that people were fully expected to live on streets. The question showed that to not live on a street was positively weird.

"Bellemonde Drive," I said. It was the closest I could get to the truth without giving a full explanation.

"Bellemonde Drive!" Paige gasped, and I suddenly realized my mistake. She thought I lived in one of the mansions on Bellemonde. Of course she'd think that. There were nothing *but* mansions on Bellemonde Drive. What had I done?

"So, you must live in one of those big Edwardian places," Paige said.

"I don't know about Edwardian," I said. "And it's not really very big. At all."

"I adore all those places on Bellemonde," Paige said.

"Mom's degree is in architecture," Bridget said. "She goes mental over old mansions."

"A bit mental," Paige admitted. "Especially Edwardian.

Even before architecture school I was in love with houses like yours."

The phone rang and Paige got up to answer it. Bridget reached for another cookie. I'd lost my appetite. I had lied! I had made Bridget and her mom think I lived in a mansion! I hadn't meant to lie. Or had I? Maybe not wanting to say the truth was the same thing as wanting to lie? I had to say something right away, I thought, as Paige hung up the phone. But when she returned to the table Paige reported that the soccer coach had just called about practice on Friday, and Bridget told Paige that she needed new cleats, and Paige told Bridget she couldn't possibly need new ones yet, and Bridget told Paige that her feet were two inches longer than they'd been four months ago, and Paige went to the mud room to inspect Bridget's cleats, and I had not said a thing.

Bridget and I went up to her room. "What do you feel like doing?" she asked, flopping on her enormous bed. She sounded exactly normal. She had no idea I'd lied. It seemed like my guilt would send out some kind of aura or vibration or something. I guess that's why I was so surprised that Bridget couldn't tell. I shouldn't have been though. After all, the whole point of dishonesty is that people not find out.

"I don't know," I said, wondering how to bring up the truth.

"Do you want to try decoding that letter?" she asked. "I've still got the pictures on my phone, if you don't have them with you."

"Actually, I wrote the whole letter out again. I've got it here," I said, sitting down beside her.

"You don't mind me helping?"

"Mind? Why would I mind?"

"In case it was secret, or something."

"No, I don't mind at all," I said. Whatever Great-great-aunt Lydia's coded letter might turn out to say, I had no intention of keeping secrets from Bridget. I was going to tell her about my treehouse, in only a moment.

"What have you tried so far?" Bridget asked, and I explained all of the code alphabets I had tried. Tell her *now*, I told myself.

"You know," Bridget said, taking the replica coded letter from me, "I'm starting to think that this letter isn't written in a coded alphabet at all."

"Really?"

"Yeah look," Bridget said. "All the words have vowels, like normal words. That wouldn't happen randomly, if your aunt whatzername had just replaced the real letters with ones from a code alphabet. Would it? Maybe it's all anagrams. You know, where the letters in every word stay the same but are rearranged? You don't mind if I write out my own copy, do you?"

"Of course not." *Now*, I told myself as Bridget hunched on the bed copying the letter. *Tell her about the treehouse now. Right now. Okay, go.* I swear that I actually opened my mouth to start, but just then Paige walked in with Bridget's clean laundry and I closed my mouth again. Bridget and I worked on anagrams, but soon realized they were not the answer. Great-great-aunt Lydia's coded letter was full of two-letter words like 'ID' and 'TE' and 'LE' and 'PE' that couldn't be rearranged into real words, and the 'X' at the end couldn't be rearranged at all. Somehow the right moment to tell Bridget that I lived in a treehouse did not come along. Late in the afternoon Paige reminded Bridget of her piano lesson. I recognized this as my cue to leave, and I collected my backpack and fleece jacket. "We'll go out by the garage door, Rosie," Paige said. "I'll give you a ride home."

"No!" I said. "No, that's okay." I could just picture Great-great-aunt Lydia swatting me away from her front gate on Bellemonde Drive while Bridget and her mom watched from the minivan. It would be horrible if they found out the truth that way. There was a puzzled silence, and I felt like I should fill it up. "Car trips of three miles or less cause half of all exhaust emissions," I said. "So I'd rather ride my bike. To reduce global warming."

"Oh." Paige smiled. "But I hate to send you riding off all by yourself when it will be getting dark soon."

"I'll be home way before dark," I said. "And I like riding all by myself. I like the quiet. It's when I meditate."

After a few more ride offers Paige let me get my bike out of the minivan. It had gotten cold, and my knuckles turned white on my handlebars. To turn what I'd just said into the truth, I tried to meditate. But my meditations never rose above one pestering thought. All my meditations were on how totally hard it was getting to tell Bridget about the treehouse.

NOTEBOOK: #15
NAME: Rosamund McGrady
SUBJECT: Fever

When it rained again three days later, I couldn't stand to return to school in my weird rain gear. I wore it out of the treehouse to avoid arguing with Mom, but when Tilley and I were getting our bikes from the shed, I stuffed my cape and gaiters in my backpack.

"You're gonna get soaked," came the voice from inside Tilley's orange plastic hood.

"Lesser of two evils," I said, and we set off on our bikes. The rain fell down from the sky and the mud sprayed up from my tires. I was oozing by the time we reached Sir Combover Elementary. When I watched Tilley scamper across the school grounds all dry and comfortable in her cape and gaiters, I almost wished I'd worn my rain gear too. But when the orange of her retreating outfit burned an afterimage onto my retina, I knew I'd made the right decision.

I got to Windward and headed for my classroom as the

warning bell rang. Devo, Matt, Heath and Zach were funneling in the doorway. Like me, they were wearing fleece jackets, but theirs were dry. They had gotten rides to school. "Hey, look what crawled out of the sewer," Devo said, and they all did their laugh track. I sneered in self-defence. A rivulet of dirty rainwater rounded the corner of my lip, and dribbled into my mouth. Miss Rankle opened up the classroom door. I went into the cloakroom and hung up my fleece jacket. A pool was forming beneath it when Kendra, Twyla and Sienna came in.

"Oh, you poor thing," Kendra said, looking me up and down. "You must feel so totally *disgusting*."

"Yeah," said Sienna. "You must feel so *gross*."

"Yeah," said Twyla. "*Revolting*. Is that how you feel?"

"Where's your special orange outfit today?" Kendra asked.

"Oh that," I said. "I just had that for the day. It's a costume."

"For what," Twyla asked.

"A play," I said.

"What's your part," asked Sienna.

"My part? Um. Radioactive waste."

"Weird play," said Twyla.

"Good casting though," said Kendra.

"Hey Matt," Devo said, lifting my jacket from its hook with the tip of somebody's furled umbrella. "Flush this back *down* the toilet, will ya?"

"Yo." Matt charged dutifully off, with my jacket speared on the umbrella. Oncoming hallway traffic scattered. Before I caught up he flung my jacket into the boys' washroom. I heard it splatter on the tiled floor.

I turned to Devo. "Get it back," I demanded. "Right now."

"Sure," Devo said. "All you've gotta do is get down on one knee and say 'I worship Devo, my Supreme Master.'"

"As if," I said.

"Okay then." Devo shrugged and walked away.

I considered running into the washroom, but fear of urinals stopped me. I went to the classroom to find Bridget, but she wasn't there. Several kids weren't there. "It seems we're decimated by *flu*," Miss Rankle said during attendance.

I couldn't wait for the day to end. Unlocking my bike after school, I was shot by rain. Coatless, I rode through a wind that could cut skin. Where the sidewalk met the path I stopped, and there I pulled my hideous cape out of my backpack. I was completely soaked, but the cape would help protect me from wind as I rode unseen through the woods. Just as I was putting it on a monstrous SUV drove by. From the passenger window Kendra looked down at me with comfortable curiosity. Cape snapping in the wind, I set off on the path through the woods. The plywood ramp over the stone wall was slippery-when-wet and I thought I'd never get over it. By the time I got to our meadow every muscle ached and I could barely climb the ladder to the treehouse.

Mom was home early that day. "Oh Rosie, look at you," she said. "How did you get so wet under your cape? Where's your jacket? Take off your things! Get into bed!"

I left my clothes in a puddle on the treehouse floor and climbed the wooden ladder. I tugged my quilt over me and flopped on my pillows, passionately in love with my bunk. Mom did not cross-examine me. She heated chicken broth on the cast-iron stove and climbed up to deliver it. The mug was nice and warm, but it seemed like way too much trouble to lift it to my mouth.

Pretty soon Dad brought Tilley home from Eveline's. Tilley was still sensibly dressed in her hideous rain gear. Dad bent at the cast-iron stove and stoked the fire. It looked not quite real, and full of strange personality. It crouched and hid, and then leapt out in surprise flames of green and neon blue. I stared until it all fell to embers. When Dad went out to chop more wood my ears vibrated with the far-away whack of the axe. I didn't climb down to the table for dinner.

The night turned to storm. On our roof, the rain burst like loud applause. The wind flung itself at the treehouse and shrieked down our chimney. Branches thrashed outside, and shadows lurched across our walls. As the treehouse rocked like a ship, I fell into a delirious sleep.

My delirium lasted three days, I was later told. I was told that my fever reached 104 degrees. A temperature of 104 degrees is enough to cause hallucinations, and supposedly I had some. Supposedly I screamed that there were pigs on my bunk, which freaked Tilley right out, even though she could plainly see that my bunk was pig-free. A temperature of 104 can cause not only hallucinations, but also permanent brain damage. It is therefore high enough to scare parents out of their wits, even casual parents like my mother. Mom and Dad were especially scared because there was no quick way of getting me to the hospital. How would they get me to the ground, they had wondered when my temperature reached its peak. In the dumbwaiter? Was that safe? And then what? Would the bike trailer take my weight? And how long would it take to haul me all the way down the path through the woods? Maybe it was better to break down Great-great-aunt Lydia's so-called electric fence so that Dad could carry me through the curly iron gate to a taxi on Bellemonde Drive? Fortunately, my fever had dropped without emergency measures.

To me the really scary part was this: when I started getting better, I heard Mom and Dad murmuring in their bunk about whether we should keep on living in the treehouse. Dad wondered whether it was responsible. I decided to recover fast, to make my parents forget all their health-and-safety concerns. I declared myself well enough to go back to school, but my parents disagreed. "No, Rosie, we'd rather err on the side of caution," Mom said, which didn't sound like her at all.

"Mom, please, please, please don't go all cautious on me," I said, rearing up from my bunk. "Don't make us move out of the treehouse. Promise me we won't."

"Did I say anything about moving out of the treehouse? We just want you to stay home from school until you've made a full recovery."

Mom and Dad went back to university, leaving me to get better on my own. I was comfortably sick. Now that I was no longer friendless, I didn't mind being alone. I nestled under my quilt, getting up only to throw another log into the cast-iron stove, or to heat myself a bowl of chicken noodle soup. I was still too weak to try decoding Great-great-aunt Lydia's letter. A lot of the time I'd just stare out my porthole, watching the oak leaves twist free and fly off in the wind. A lot of the time I thought how pleasant it was to be away from Devo and Matt and Heath and Zach and Twyla and Nova and Sienna and Kendra.

For six entire days I did not leave the treehouse, not even to go to the bathroom. As an emergency alternative to the outhouse, the treehouse porch had what medieval castle-dwellers called a garderobe. "Garderobe" is just a fancy name for what is basically a hole in the porch. The fancy name does not help. A garderobe feels as primitive as it is. On day six I felt well enough to go back to using the outhouse. Over my pyjamas I put on the fleece jacket that Mom had retrieved from the Windward lost and found. I climbed down the ladder and crossed the meadow for the first time in a week.

It was only when I was coming back from the outhouse that I saw something weird on the trunk of the oak tree. It was a bunch of dead plants, tied with a blue satin ribbon. The ribbon was skewered to the trunk with a small pocket knife. I stared, wondering when the bunch had been put there. Recently, I concluded. Very recently, or my family would have seen it while they were coming or going. I turned and looked around the meadow, but there was no sign of life. I pulled the knife from the bark and took the dead plants. There was more than one kind, but I didn't recognize any of them. I sniffed at them cautiously. They smelled better than they looked. There was a whiff of something familiar. I stood straining to place it, the way you strain for a name that's on the tip of your tongue. But I couldn't get it.

I folded the knife into my jacket pocket, and stuck the

dead plants there too. I climbed to the treehouse and got back in my bunk. If Great-great-aunt Lydia wanted nothing to do with me or my family, I wondered, why had she brought us dead plants? It was a very weird thing to do.

I got both of Great-great-aunt Lydia's letters from my wallet. I read the letter Great-great-aunt Lydia had written in code, and I wondered about the word 'CHHARM'. I read the letter Great-great-aunt Lydia had torn up and thrown in the stream. For the first time, I felt a twinge of the creepiness that Tilley felt about Great-great-aunt Lydia. For the first time, I wondered if my description of her as some kind of witch was entirely my own invention. Reading the torn blue strip, I wondered if it was about an *incant*ation, someday soon.

| NOTEBOOK: | #16 |
| --- | --- |
| NAME: | Rosamund McGrady |
| SUBJECT: | The Fight |

When I displayed unmistakable symptoms of health I was sent off to school again. I had dropped Tilley off and was a half a mile away from Windward when I spotted Devo. He was up ahead, riding his bike on the sidewalk, helmet dangling from his handlebars. There was a huge black Range Rover driving right beside him. The driver was a dark-skinned lady who yelled at Devo through the open passenger window. "Devon," she yelled with a really heavy accent. "Devon! Helmet! Your helmet! Helmet Devon! Devon! Devon! Helmet! Helmet! I tell your mother! You hear me? Tell your mother!"

Devo had a nanny! From the way he pretended not to hear her, I guessed he was embarrassed. I caught up to him and coasted along. "Helmet, helmet Devon," I said. I admit that this was not the slightest bit clever, but as long as it bugged him I really didn't care. And it did bug him, too. I know because of the two words that he said back to me. I won't repeat them in this notebook.

"Better not swear," I said. "Or your *nanny* will wash your mouth out with soap." Unsupervised, I pedaled ahead to Windward.

I joined the rest of my class in the hallway, where they waited for Miss Rankle to open the door. Kendra, Twyla, Nova and Sienna were together; Bridget was off by herself. She came to meet me. "You're back," she said. "Finally." When Miss Rankle opened the classroom door, Bridget and I got bunched together with Nova and Twyla and Sienna and Kendra, but none of them spoke. Kendra just raised her chin and swirled her hair, and the others did too, as well as their inferior hair would allow.

"What's with *them*," I asked Bridget. She shook her head and rolled her eyes, but she didn't explain. Creative writing was long and slow. Miss Rankle assigned a short story written from the viewpoint of an inanimate object. This did not interest me. The only thing that interested me at the moment was the fight between Bridget and Kendra. I could hardly wait until recess to get the details.

"So, how come Kendra isn't talking to you?" I asked Bridget before the recess bell had even stopped ringing.

"'Cause I won't talk back," Bridget replied. "What are you gonna do for your short story?"

"Not sure. So why aren't you talking to Kendra?"

Bridget shrugged and shook her head, to show she didn't want to talk about it. "My story's going to be about a diary," she said. "This really frustrated diary. Like, the girl who owns the diary writes all her secrets and problems in it, right? And the diary can see that this girl is making some really big mistakes and the diary is just so totally dying to give her advice, but it can't, cause it's only inanimate, right?"

"That sounds good," I said. "What are her problems?"

"Haven't got that far yet," Bridget said.

"How about—she has a fight with a friend. That would be so interesting. A fight with a mean, snobby, popular friend."

"Yeah, maybe," was all Bridget said, and the whole rest of the day she did not mention Kendra.

When the final bell rang Bridget walked me to the bike rack.

"Are you going out for Halloween this year?" she asked as I unlocked my bike.

"I guess. Are you?"

"Definitely. I figure it might be my last year. My parents think I'm getting too old. It's so unfair. Last year I was supposedly too young to go out without a parent, and next year I'm supposedly too old to go out at all. So I've gotta make this year count. Want to come with me?"

"You and—"

"Just me."

"Sure."

"Should I ask my mom if you can sleep over? Since Halloween's a Friday?"

"Okay," I said. I wrapped my cable lock around my crossbar and straddled my bike.

"Give me your number and I'll call you later." As Bridget was writing my cell number on a crumpled test paper, I saw Devo on his bike, way across the school grounds. I saw him but I paid no attention. He was meaningless at that distance. He bicycled toward us and then he entered my mental radar screen. I never realized before how much body language there is in bike riding. Devo was hunched and he was fast and he was, I somehow knew, full of criminal intent. He was close and he was speeding straight at us. He set a collision course. He tensed for the smash. Bridget fled in alarm, but I was stuck straddling my bike. Adrenalin jounced through me and I did something stupid. I screamed. I screamed, even though Devo had actually braked a split second earlier. I screamed, because I was too busy panicking to process the fact that he'd already stopped. I screamed, and everybody who turned to look saw I was terrified of a guy standing still over his bike, smiling.

Of course his smile wasn't genuine. Devo never really smiled, just smirked. His mouth gave a farewell twist and he rode away down the hill, jumping over a little dirt bump at the bottom. His bike flew a bit off the ground. He made a tight turn and braked, totally pleased with himself.

Beyond the bottom of the hill the ground tilted up a couple of yards to the basketball court. It tilted really steeply: not quite straight up and down, but almost. As Devo stood there thinking how great he was, I buckled my helmet. "Talk to you tonight, then," I said to Bridget.

"Bye," she called as I pedaled down the hill.

"Chicken," Devo yelled, when I didn't aim for his stupid little jump. I pedaled until the pedals spun uselessly. I blurred down that hill and braced myself for what was coming. Except that you never realize just how steep a steep thing is until you're actually on it, and that's how it was with the rise to the basketball court. As my bike swooped up the rise I couldn't see anything but sky. Then my wheels left the ground and I was *in* the sky. I couldn't have been in the air more than a couple of seconds, but it was long enough to worry about landing. My front tire dropped. The sky vanished. The basketball court appeared. It rushed at me like a giant fly swatter. My front tire hit the concrete hard, then my back tire. My bike wobbled like crazy, and that was the scariest moment. But all that practice launching myself over Great-great-aunt Lydia's stone wall paid off. I was still riding. I turned my bike and braked.

I was trying hard to control my face, which wanted to do a big obnoxious grin. Devo was trying hard to control his face too, to act like he wasn't impressed. For sure he was, though, because other people had their mouths hanging open. Up at the top of the hill, Bridget was grinning the way I was trying not to. I waved at her and she waved back. Then, with jelly-legs, I rode off toward the treehouse, the cool one for a change.

NOTEBOOK: #17

NAME: Rosamund McGrady

SUBJECT: Hallowed Evening

I couldn't think of a Halloween costume. We had no dress-up things at all at the treehouse. We didn't even have any old clothes to paint or glue things onto. “Mom, I still don't have a costume,” I complained as she worked at the folding table.

“No? You'll figure something out,” Mom replied, rewinding her battery-operated CD player. She replayed gorilla grunts and scribbled something down.

“But we've got nothing to make it out of. We should buy some costume stuff.”

“Buy costume stuff! Where are we going to store costume stuff, in a treehouse? Just use your imagination,” Mom said, exactly as expected.

“I can't use *just* imagination—I'll be naked. I at least need some actual clothes to apply my imagination *to*.”

“You'll be fine,” Mom said. “You know Rosie, I've got to mail this grant proposal before November first, so it would be a real help if you'd make Tilley's costume too." I sighed and muttered and grumbled and headed down the treehouse ladder to look for costume materials. I wandered the grounds, trying to figure out how to make costumes out of rocks or tree stumps. Eventually I thought of more suitable materials. Tilley could be a scarecrow stuffed with meadow grass. I could be a bag of groceries, made of boxes and jugs and stuff from our household recycling.

I made the costumes on Halloween after school, as darkness fell. A big autumn moon rose through the bare oak branches, up toward the clouds. Tilley and I got into costume and waited for Mom and Dad to get home.

"You know what we should do," I said as I painted Tilley's triangle nose. "We should trick-or-treat at Grand Oak Manor, and see what it looks like inside." The dead plants had made me more curious than ever about Great-great-aunt Lydia. I still hadn't figured out what kind they were. My parents, as scientists, probably could have identified them, but I'd kept their discovery secret. If Dad was having second thoughts about the safety of the treehouse, I didn't want to tell him about weird stuff happening. And stabbing dead plants to our tree was definitely weird. The more I thought about it, the more it seemed like an act of voodoo. I liked this idea. It was creepily thrilling to think that Great-great-aunt Lydia was a practicing witch. Since she was going to be our enemy, I wanted her to be an interesting one. I wanted her to be wicked. Her voodoo or witchcraft or whatever did not scare me. Nothing had ever happened, up to that point in my life, to make me believe in the occult.

"I'm not trick-or-treating at Grand Oak Manor," Tilley answered. "It's scary in there."

"Oh, come on, Tilley," I said. "I was just making all that stuff up, about the man-eating fish and the deer being turned into a tree. You know that."

"I know, but it's still scary. Cause Great-great-aunt Lydia doesn't like us."

"She won't know who we are. We'll be in costume. We'll be disguised."

"A triangle nose is a bad disguise."

"So I'll draw a scarecrow face on a grocery bag and put it over your head. I'll do one for me too. It's a great spying opportunity Tilley. Any real spy would jump at the chance."

"I'm not gonna be a spy anymore. I'm gonna be an astronaut."

"Well, when you apply to be an astronaut they're going to test you for bravery. So you may as well start practicing now."

I stepped through the arched doorway and got two brown paper grocery bags from the recycling box on our porch.

"What are you doing?" Tilley asked.

"Making your scarecrow head."

"I don't *want* to trick-or-treat at Great-great-aunt Lydia's." Tilley stuck out her lower lip for emphasis.

"If you don't want to you don't have to. We'll just go down to the gap in the fence."

"Why?"

"You're not scared to stand outside the fence, are you?"

"No."

"Well," I said illogically. "That's why we're going."

I made our heads and folded them into my cargo pocket. We strapped on our headlamps and descended through the trap door. It's a bit dangerous going down a ladder in the dark as a bag of groceries, and I was glad when my feet touched the ground.

"Switch off your headlamp, Tilley," I said. "In honour of Halloween." Guided by the amber moon, we crossed the meadow. A raccoon hunched along ahead of us, looking suspiciously over its shoulder before veering off toward the stream. We reached Great-great-aunt Lydia's fence, and felt our way along to the loose board. I swung it to one side. There was a light on in the turret at Grand Oak Manor, and another one down on the main floor.

"Great-great-aunt Lydia must *want* trick-or-treaters, Tilley," I said. "Otherwise she'd switch off all the lights. That's what anti-Halloween people do." As we peered through the fence gap, clouds swallowed up the moon. Suddenly all was darkness, except for the few golden windows of Grand Oak Manor.

"I can't see," Tilley said.

"Which is perfect," I said. "Cause neither can Great-great-aunt Lydia. We'll get all the way to her front doorstep without her seeing. She'll think we came from Bellemonde Drive, like the other trick-or-treaters." I stuck one foot through the gap in the fence.

"You said we were staying outside the fence."

"You can stay here, if you want. I'm going in." My grocery costume stuck in the gap until I shifted my contents. I peered through my cut-out eye holes. It was hard to see, but the bushes were one shade darker than the dark beyond. They were just visible enough for us to guess at the path. Holding Tilley's scarecrow arm, I led us half-blindly toward the front of Grand Oak Manor. When I saw the darker darkness of the deer-shaped tree, I knew we were getting close.

A weird smell wafted up my nostrils. It was sweet, and musky, and smoldering. I'd never smelled anything like it before. As I stood inhaling, I saw a tiny red glow suspended in the darkness beyond the deer tree. The glow flared, then dwindled. My eye holes shifted, and when I got them back the glow was gone. But from the same area came a single dry cough. I leaned down to Tilley's bag head. "Tilley," I whispered into the paper of my own bag. "There's someone there."

"What?" Tilley's bag head crinkled. "I can't hear you."

I plucked off my own head. "There's someone *there*," I whispered again, tugging her stuffed meadow grass arm. We turned and ran, snagging bushes in our hurry. I tried to listen behind myself, but the shifting of my groceries was louder than any pursuing footsteps would have been. We slipped through the fence gap and swung the board shut behind us. I switched on my headlamp so we could run faster, but I didn't pause again until we reached our oak tree.

"I *told* you it was scary in there," Tilley accused from the treehouse porch as I climbed through the trap door. I felt bad for bringing Tilley into the Manor garden, because actually, it *had* been scary. Why was Great-great-aunt Lydia lurking out there in the pitch black garden? And what had she been silently thinking, as she listened to us approach? What was the glow? And what was that weird smell? I got my bunch of dead plants out of my bunk cupboard and broke off a handful. "What are you doing?" Tilley asked, as I dropped the dead plants onto the cast-iron stove. I held a match to them.

"Smell that," I said, as they smoked, then flamed. "Is that what we just smelled in the garden?"

Tilley sniffed. "Sort of," she said. "But sort of not. That smell in the garden was creepy. Really creepy."

"Yeah," I said. I swept the ashes into the stove, deciding that it was time to restore a wholesome atmosphere. "Want to play checkers 'til it's time to go out?" I asked. We did, and Tilley brightened right back to normal. Tilley tends to get over things quickly.

During our second game I saw the LED lights of my parents' bikes flickering along the meadow. "Right down," I called from the porch. We met them at the shed, and the four of us rode off across the dark meadow. Our bicycle headlights swooped through the night. I tingled with adrenalin. Part of the adrenalin was from the scare in the Manor garden, and part was from suspense about what was going to happen later. Because that night, definitely, without fail, one hundred percent for sure, I was going to tell Bridget about the treehouse. It was my unspoken vow.

We reached the end of the woods and entered the world of sidewalks and houses and streetlights. Pumpkin smiles flickered at us as we rode through the wispy Halloween air. A few streets later we reached Bridget's house. "This is it," I said, wheeling my bike into her front yard.

"Goodness," said Mom.

"Imposing," said Dad.

Bridget opened the door. She was a mosquito, with coat hanger wings, and sieves for eyes, and a paper towel tube for a proboscis, and a half-inflated red balloon for a drop of blood. Her parents came up behind her and introduced themselves to Mom and Dad. This was a moment of danger. With Paige being so mental about Edwardian houses, there was high risk that she would say something about the mansion. If she did, Mom and Dad would look all confused and blurt out that we lived in a treehouse, because I had never told them about the misunderstanding. I'd known that there was no way to explain it to my parents without triggering a lecture about pretending to be something I wasn't.

The conversation on Bridget's doorstep was about, if I've got this right, the latest resolutions of the Parents' Advisory Committee. It was so boring that I wondered how even grown-ups could stand to talk about it, but I was paying close attention, in case the topic suddenly switched to mansions. If it did, I was going to create a distraction by falling down in a pretend faint. I thought that this would be hard to do realistically, and painful, and damaging to my costume, so I was relieved when Mom and Dad kissed me goodbye and rode off with Tilley toward Eveline's.

Paige briefed us on Halloween safety. "Now what are you going to do?" Paige asked Bridget, in review.

"We're going to hitchhike to the convenience store and accept drugs from strangers. Honestly, Mom, what do you think we're going to do? We're going trick-or-treating. We'll avoid flames and explosives and we'll look for cars before we cross the street. We'll be fine." And out we went.

It was my most profitable Halloween ever. In my old neighbourhood people gave out teeny chocolate bars; and homemade stuff like popcorn balls that we'd throw away in case of poison or razor blades; and Halloween kisses made of industrial adhesive. In Bridget's neighbourhood we got great stuff. We were on our way from a house that had just given us each a full-size chocolate bar *and* a bag of chips when Bridget said "Look at that." She pointed to a winged dragon that was walking toward us.

"That's like something from special—" I was about to say 'effects' when the dragon threw something at my feet. I screamed at the first explosion, and again as the firecracker ricocheted along the walkway. There is something humiliating about screaming, at least when the scream isn't followed up with an actual 911-type emergency. It all felt familiar. I marched to the dragon and there, inside its jaws, behind its fangs, was Devon Radcliffe. Beside him were three bed-sheet ghosts, all rumpling up with laughter.

"You idiot," I yelled. "That's dangerous. Didn't your *nanny* teach you that."

"My *what*?" Devo said.

"Nanny. Nanny. Your nanny." I spotted her at the curb, in the driver's seat of the black Range Rover, her face floating among the reflections on the driver's side window. I pointed. "Her."

"Her? You mean my *driver*."

"Driver? Good spin, Devo. Nice try. But we all know a nanny when we see one."

"So watcha got here," Devo said, yanking my pillowcase. "Candied slugs?" As I snatched at it he turned and peered inside. "Mars bars, chips. A bit normal for you, isn't it?" He dropped the pillowcase on the walkway. I crouched to get the stuff he'd spilled.

"Don't go to her house," Devo called to other trick-or-treaters, pointing down at me. "They're giving out slugs."

I straightened up. "You are so boring," I said. "Is that the only joke you can think of?"

"Who's joking? Where is your house, anyway? I bet it's straight out of the Adams Family."

"Yeah right. It's only on *Bellemonde Drive*," Bridget said. It made me feel a bit sick to hear her bragging to our arch-enemy about my mansion. That could only make it harder for her to find out, later that night, that I actually lived in a treehouse.

"Well whoop-de-do," was what Devo said.

"Come on Bridget," I said. "Let's not waste our time talking to this loser." With as much dignity as a mosquito and a bag of groceries could manage, we marched away. On the opposite sidewalk we saw Kendra (witch), with Twyla (scuba diver), Sienna (right half angel, left half devil), and Nova (pirate queen). They didn't say hi, and we didn't either. Bridget and I stood shoulder-to-shoulder consulting our custom-made trick-or-treat map, and went off on our own special route. Our route was ambitious, and the candy massed in our pillowcases like treasure in a chest. After awhile my arms ached with the weight of it. I was cold too, and I didn't mind when Bridget asked, three quarters of the way through our route, if I would mind going home.

At her place we changed into pyjamas and poured our landslides of candy onto her bedroom carpet. We took turns choosing until it was all divided. Then we each separated our treats into three broad categories: chocolate bars, candies and savoury items. We then sub-divided each category. Chocolate bars were separated into plain milk; plain dark; containing fruit or nut bits; containing creamy or semi-liquid filling; containing chewy centre; containing biscuit or crispy centre; etc. There was a lot of debate about categories, so it took forever. Then when everything had been properly classified we made detailed inventories, to protect our stashes from family members.

"Almost midnight girls," Paige said, sticking her head around Bridget's door. "Lights out, I think." While Bridget used her bathroom I flipped through the photo album that was open on her bedside table. It started when Bridget was a baby, looking just like millions of other babies. In the following pages her Bridget-ness emerged. There was a picture of Bridget on the beach, holding hands with another little girl. The other little girl was Kendra. Kendra appeared over and over on the following pages, as she and Bridget gradually turned into their present-day selves. Kendra and Bridget in early Halloween costumes; Kendra and Bridget on a dock; Kendra and Bridget with Easter baskets; Kendra and Bridget on Santa's knee. Finally, there were four poses of Kendra and Bridget making faces in one of those curtained booths at the shopping mall.

When Bridget and I got into her bed and switched off the lava lamp, we rated the Halloween costumes we'd seen. Devo got ten out of ten points for visual impact, but he was penalized eight points for having bought his costume ready made. This gave him a final score of two out of ten. Only a fraction of my mind was on costume ratings, because I was about to tell Bridget about the treehouse. I had actually written a rough draft of my speech in a notebook, and I had rehearsed it out loud alone in the treehouse. Now I was about to actually deliver it. It would be hard to start, but if I stayed focused, all of a sudden I'd just do it. It would be like the first time on the rope swing. Before I knew it, it would be over.

"Kendra I'd give maybe three points for neatness," Bridget was saying, "but zero for imagination. I mean, a witch? That's lame."

"Bridget," I asked. "What happened with you and Kendra?"

"What happened? Well, I'm mad at her. I dumped her."

"I know that, but why?"

"Because she's a liar," Bridget said. "That's why."

"Yeah." I paused. "So, what did she lie about?"

"All that stuff about *Clean Getaway*," Bridget said. "And her big acting debut. That was all such a bunch of lies."

"How do you know?"

"The Smithereens," Bridget said. "They said that the whole time they were on holiday in L.A., she just hung around the set of *Out of Nowhere* until she finally got to be in one single solitary crowd scene. An unpaid extra. And the Smithereens said when you watch the crowd scene you can't even pick her out. *Clean Getaway* isn't even a real movie."

"Who are the Smithereens?"

"Her brothers and sisters. The other five Smith kids," Bridget said. "Yeah, Kendra totally lied to me. That's why I dumped her."

I would have been delighted to say that it was completely, horribly, sinfully, unforgivably terrible of Kendra to lie, if only I wasn't just about to tell Bridget that I had lied myself.

"So, did you tell Kendra what the Smithereens said?" I asked.

"Yes. And she tried to say she hadn't lied at all, it was all a misunderstanding, it was all just me getting the wrong idea or something. Which is a total insult to my intelligence. It made me even madder."

"Wow. So. Why do you figure she said all that stuff?" I asked.

"To show off. Her specialty."

"Hmm."

"What?" Bridget asked.

"Well. I don't know. Just—whatever you liked about Kendra before all the showbiz lies, don't you still like that stuff about her?" I definitely did not want to talk Bridget into being friends with Kendra again, but I had to find out the answer.

Bridget thought. "Not really. No. Like, when somebody lies and you find out, every single thing they say seems like a lie after that. And you look at them, and all of a sudden they seem all creepy. Like they've murdered your friend and taken over the body or something. I don't know, it's just—creepy."

I exhaled slowly. Omigosh, that was close! My confession had been right on the tip of my tongue! A few more seconds and it would have been out in the sound waves! Thank goodness I had found out, just in the nick of time, that I could never, ever, ever tell Bridget that I had lied about where I lived.

We talked about other things. After awhile Bridget

was mumbling, and then she was asleep. I stayed awake beside her, listening to the screech of fireworks, and then to the silence of the long night.

I was tired the next morning when we had our breakfast of Mars Bars, cheese puffs and orange juice. I was even more tired later, riding back to the treehouse with my Halloween loot in my backpack. When I climbed the ladder I saw there was nobody home. A note from Mom and Dad said they were picking Tilley up at Eveline's.

I climbed to my bunk. I flopped there and stared out my porthole, watching the very last of the oak leaves fly slowly away. My thoughts kept going around and around in my mind, coming back exactly the same again and again. Bridget hated liars. Because she hated liars, I could never tell her the truth, because the truth was that I'd lied. Because I'd lied, I would have to keep on lying. Lying was the way to make sure Bridget liked me, because Bridget hated liars. Something seemed very wrong with this logic, yet no matter how hard I tried I couldn't come up with another strategy for keeping Bridget as a friend.

NOTEBOOK: #18

NAME: Rosamund McGrady

SUBJECT: Pitch Black

By November it was pouring rain almost every day. Going to school without my rain gear was impossible, but so was wearing it around Kendra and gang. My solution was to wear it on the long ride through the woods and take it off when I got near the sidewalk. "Okay Tilley," I said, braking my bike near the end of the path. "We'll lock our bikes here. Take off your cape and we'll put them in this hollow tree."

"How come we're taking off our capes?"

"Cause we're superheroes."

"But superheroes *wear* capes."

"Not all the time they don't. Think about it. Real superheroes have human identities too. And when they're in their human identities, they're actually really careful to be all capeless and normal."

"Like Superman,"Tilley considered.

"Like Superman," I agreed.

Tilley nodded thoughtfully and took off her cape. “Aren’t we gonna get wet?” she asked as I finished locking up our bikes.

“I brought umbrellas,” I said. “For our human identities.”

Tilley smiled secretively as she accepted her umbrella. At the end of the path we peered through the criss-cross of twigs to the sidewalk. “Pop out when nobody’s coming?” Tilley asked.

“Exactly,” I said, and Tilley leapt onto the sidewalk as though it were the far side of a crevasse. I put up the umbrellas and we walked the rest of the way to our schools, arriving pretty much dry.

Most days I went to Bridget’s after school. We spent a lot of time trying to figure out Great-great-aunt Lydia’s coded letter. One afternoon Bridget said, “Maybe this isn’t written in a code at all. Maybe it’s written in a secret *language*. That could explain why all the words have vowels in the right places.”

“But it’s almost like the language is English,” I said. “‘NO’ and ‘USE’ and ‘SOB’ and ‘TIN’ are actual English words. And there’s more if you count wrong spellings. ‘CHHARM’ and ‘EATTEN.’ So how can English be part of a secret language?”

“Could it be some kind of ancient English,” Bridget suggested.

“The Oxford English Dictionary has ancient English,” I said.

We got the OED out of Paige’s office and looked up the words one by one.

“‘ID’ means unconscious impulses,” Bridget

announced. "Urges that you don't even know that you have."

"So it *is* English," I said. "And 'NO' means no, obviously."

"'TE' is a chemical symbol for the element tellurium."

"What would that mean in a sentence though? The unconscious urge to avoid that element?"

"I don't know," Bridget said. "And 'VERTHIN' isn't an English word. Shoot. The dictionary goes straight from 'vertex' to 'vertical'."

I flipped the dictionary's pages. "'KAPA's not *exactly* a word," I reported, "but if you spell it with two 'P's it's the tenth letter of the Greek alphabet."

We were looking up 'IROFSCIS' when Paige came in. "Twenty minutes 'til your piano lesson Bridget," she said. "Rosie, I'll drive you home."

"Oh, no, that's okay. It's not raining that hard. I'll walk. I love to walk," I said. "I find raindrops on my face so refreshing."

"I know, Rosie," Paige said. "But I can't let you do that. It's dark out." I looked out the window and discovered she was right. Daylight savings had ended, and at five o'clock, it was dark as midnight.

"Oh, darkness doesn't bother me," I said. "I like darkness. I love darkness. I adore it."

"But Rosie—"

"And I hate causing carbon emissions. And I need the exercise. And the meditation time," I said.

"I know you do. But it's pitch black out and it's not safe for you to walk. I'm driving you." Paige's voice was firm.

Could I excuse myself and climb out the bathroom

window or something? No, I thought. That would make a bad impression. "Okay," I said slowly. Slowly I put on my fleece jacket and slowly I walked to the garage, trying to think of some way out of this. Sitting beside Bridget in the back seat of the minivan, I felt as desperate as a kidnap victim. The automatic garage door rolled itself away and we drove into the pouring rain. My mind was flapping like the windshield wipers, but I couldn't think of any way out of that minivan that Paige would agree to. And so, a few minutes later, we pulled onto Bellemonde Drive.

"This is good," I said, a block before Great-great-aunt Lydia's. "You can let me off here."

"Which house is yours?" Bridget asked.

"It's just on the next block," I said. "But this is fine, really. I'll get out here."

"No, I'll bring you," Paige said, and she drove on. On that whole next block Great-great-aunt Lydia's was the only house.

"This one?" Paige asked as Grand Oak Manor filled up the minivan windows.

"Mm-hm," I answered.

"*This* is your house?" Paige asked, staring out the window.

"WOW," said Bridget. "COOL! It's like a *castle*! Those towers are *awesome*! LUCKY!!!"

I couldn't wait to get out of there. "Thank you for the ride," I said, wrenching open the minivan door. "Thank you for having me." I slid the door shut. After a few steps I turned and waved to signal that they should go. They waved back, but Paige did a "shoo along" thing with her fingers. I knew what this meant. It meant they were going to wait until I was at the door.

I stood outside the curly iron gate of Grand Oak Manor. The lighted Manor windows glared down at me. Rain wet my scalp and dribbled under my collar as I rattled in the dark at the gate's catch. I hoped Paige would lose patience and drive off, but she didn't. When I swung the creaking gate inward, the minivan was still there. I walked through the rain up the Manor walkway, slowly, to give myself time to think of all that could go wrong. But soon I'd spent the distance of the walkway. I was at the bottom of the Manor's big stone steps. I had no choice but to climb them. As I reached the porch a light came on. I nearly jumped out of my skin. Then I realized that a motion detector, not a person, had turned it on. I waved at the minivan again, expecting Paige to drive off now that I was safely on a well-lit porch. She didn't. I waved harder, but the minivan still didn't move. With horror, I realized that Paige was going to wait until I was actually *in the house*.

What was I going to do? If I just stood there, Paige would come out of the minivan to see what was wrong. That could bring her face to face with Great-great-aunt Lydia. To make Paige and Bridget go away, I somehow had to get inside. I put my hand to the door knocker, which was shaped like a woman's face. The door knocker had snaky metal hair and looked unfriendly. With no idea what would happen next, I knocked three loud knocks. A long silence gave me time to panic. I heard movement. The door swung open, and there, a foot away, was Great-great-aunt Lydia. People were shorter in the olden days, and my face was level with hers. It was a wrinkled, unsmiling face with staring dull eyes. Her veiny hand clutched the door. *She's about to slam it on me*, I thought. I couldn't let that happen. I stepped over the threshold and threw my arms around her.

"Great-great-aunt Lydia," I said, because it felt too weird to say nothing. "It's me, your great-great-niece, Rosamund." I felt her move. I wondered if she might try to overpower me, and I hugged her harder. She felt squishy, and sort of loose in her skin, like a giant bag of prunes. She had a complicated smell that I couldn't quite identify. It was sort of like the inside of old suitcases, sort of like lavender.

From the corner of my eye I saw the minivan pull away. When the tail lights were gone I whirled away from Great-great-aunt Lydia and ran down the steps. It felt weird, though, to run away from a person I had just hugged. I turned around. Great-great-aunt Lydia was still there, lit up by the porch light. Her embroidered cardigan was damp from my hug. She stared at me hard.

"Goodbye," I said.

"Rosamund." She spoke in a strange voice. I fled before she could say or do anything to me. I ran past the deer-shaped tree and the man-eating-fish pond, toward the gap in the fence that would return me to the tree-house.

NOTEBOOK: #19

NAME: Rosamund McGrady

SUBJECT: Excuses

"That's quite a house you live in," Paige said the next day at Bridget's. "Grand Oak Manor! I looked it up in *Our Architectural History*." She put a plate of brownies on the table.

"Grand Oak Manor is in a book? Really?" I asked.

"You didn't know?" Paige asked. "I thought you'd have a copy on your coffee table."

"Huh?" Bridget's brownie stopped midway to her mouth. "That place we dropped you off is Grand Oak Manor? Grand Oak Manor is *your* house? I thought it was your great-aunt whatzername who lived at Grand Oak Manor. Lydia Florence Augustine. The one your family had the big fight with."

"Ummm." I couldn't help sighing, realizing I had to lie again. "No. Actually, no. Great-great-aunt Lydia doesn't live there."

"But that's what her stationery says," Bridget said. "On

the letter we're decoding. I remember it from my cell phone pictures. Lydia Florence Augustine McGrady, Grand Oak Manor, Number 9 Bellemonde Drive."

"Yeah," I said. "Yeah, but that stationery is old. Great-great-aunt Lydia *used* to live at Grand Oak Manor. Before the split in the family. Before she ran away."

"I can't believe you didn't tell me this before!" Bridget put her brownie down. She still hadn't taken a bite. "If she ran away from Grand Oak Manor when the family split up, and you found the letter at Grand Oak Manor, then of course the letter's old. It's obvious!"

"Oh, yeah," I said cluelessly.

"A big split in the family?" asked Paige. "There's nothing about *that* in my book."

"What *does* your book say about Grand Oak Manor?" I asked. I needed to know. I was finding out that lying is harder than other kinds of making things up. In creative writing, for example, you can make up whatever you want. Lies, however, must be carefully designed to fit together with fact.

Paige told us what the book said. My great-great-grandfather, Magnus, the lumber baron, had bought the Grand Oak grounds to log them, but when his bride fell in love with the property he built the Manor instead. He liked to show off his wealth, according to the book, so he spared no expense, and when the Manor was finished he had lots and lots of fancy parties. After his children Lydia and Tavish were born, Magnus showed off some more by building the largest treehouse in North America.

"It sounds amazing," Paige said. "A real cottage in a tree! You must know something about the treehouse, Rosie."

They loved the sound of the treehouse. They wanted to know more about the treehouse. There would never be a better chance to tell Paige and Bridget that I lived in the treehouse. And my urge to tell them was strong. Lying was so stressful. But lying, like everything else, gathers its own momentum. Once you start it's hard to stop. What words would I use to introduce the truth? There was no time to compose. My response was overdue. "Umm," I said. "Yeah. I think I've heard something about it."

"So it's not there anymore. It wasn't clear from *Our Architectural History*. It just gives the past, not the present."

"Too bad the treehouse is gone," Bridget said. "That would be the coolest thing ever. Wouldn't you just love it, Rosie? Can you imagine how much fun we'd have up there?"

"Yeah," I said. I could totally imagine how much fun we'd have up there, if I hadn't gone and screwed everything up.

"The Manor looks pretty cool too, though," Bridget said. "Those little turrets look so cozy."

"Umm," I said. "Yeah, I guess."

"Do you have those hidden passageways for servants?"

"Umm," I said. "Yeah."

"Cool!" Bridget said. "My house is so new and boring. I want to see *your* house. Let's go there tomorrow."

"Umm. Yeah. Except that my parents stay out at the university every day until dinnertime, and they won't let me have friends over unless they're home. They're, like, over-the-top paranoid strict."

"Really," Paige said. "I wouldn't have guessed it from meeting them."

"What about your grandma," Bridget said. "Can't you have friends over when she's there?"

"My grandma? My grandma isn't there."

"Well, who was that old lady you were hugging when we drove you home?" Bridget meant Great-great-aunt Lydia. "Oh," I said. "Oh. My grandma. She was there *yesterday*. But she isn't there anymore. She's. . . ."

"She's from out of town?" Bridget asked, just as I was about to say, "She's dead."

"Out of town, yeah," I said. "She's from out of town."

As November wore on, I realized that I needed another excuse for not inviting Bridget over. My parents staying out at the university until dinnertime explained why I couldn't invite her after school. But what about Saturdays and Sundays? What explanation could there be for never, ever, *ever* inviting her over?

All the explanations I came up with had problems. Like, that I had an uncle living in the mansion, who was nice most of the time, but who ran around waving a meat cleaver when he was drunk, or on drugs, or insane, or in a really bad mood. But that explanation might make Paige call the child protection authorities. Or how about that my house had been quarantined because a family member, maybe the same pretend uncle, had cholera or SARS or black plague? But if that was true, I wouldn't be allowed to go outside myself, would I?

Then one Saturday the explanation came to me. Bridget and I had been making fudge out of sweetened condensed milk and melted chocolate. We were cleaning up the kitchen when Paige opened the office door and came into the family room off the kitchen. "Well, it feels good to have that done," she said, switching on the gas fireplace. "I finally finished the plans for my client's renovation." Renovations, I thought! Why hadn't I thought of that before?

"We're renovating too," I said. "I keep wanting to have Bridget over. But Mom says I can't until our renovations are finished."

Paige turned from the gas fireplace. "You're renovating?" she cried. "What renovations are you doing?"

I hadn't thought that far ahead. I stood at the kitchen sink, staring. "We're making a family room," I said. "By the kitchen. With a gas fireplace."

"Are you expanding out the back? Or just taking out an interior wall?"

"Umm. Interior wall?"

"Oh, good. It would be a crime to change the exterior."

"Yeah. No. Just that interior wall thing. But the reno is one big disaster area."

"Well, yours is a big house, lucky for you. A kitchen reno still leaves you with lots of livable space."

"No, it's all pretty unlivable, actually. There are power tools all over the place. Like, everywhere. Just waiting to saw an arm off."

"So you're doing more than just a kitchen reno, then?"

"Ummm. I guess. Yeah."

"What if we just ran around in the secret hidden passageways," Bridget suggested. "Away from all the construction."

"Hmmm. Well. Actually. Actually, I think we might be renovating the hidden passageways, too." I sounded like an idiot.

Paige went upstairs then and Bridget and I got out our copies of Great-great-aunt Lydia's coded letter. "Let's look up 'SORSCO'," Bridget said, taking the dictionary from the bookshelf. "I bet it has something to do with sorcery."

"That would fit," I said. I was thinking about Great-great-aunt Lydia burning weird stuff in the garden on Halloween night, and about the bunch of dead plants she'd stabbed to the tree.

"Why?" Bridget asked, and I remembered that she didn't know about those things. I hadn't told her because there was no way of doing it without a lot more complicated lying.

"Umm," I said. "It would fit with the word 'CHHAR-M'."

"Yeah," she said. "It would." But SORSCO wasn't in the dictionary. 'ULDDO' wasn't either. Neither was 'SOMU'.

"Bridget, I have to get going," I said, as she flipped through the OED. Outside the kitchen window the sky was darkening. Ever since the time that Paige had driven me up to Great-great-aunt Lydia's front gate, I'd been careful to leave Bridget's place before nightfall.

"Right this minute?" Bridget asked.

"Sorry, but yeah. I have to go. My parents said I had to be home by . . ." What time was it anyway? "By right about now. You know how they are. Crazy strict. I can't be late."

"My mom will probably drive you."

"No!"

"Oh right, carbon emissions, right? Okay, I'll check the fudge." Bridget opened the fridge and tested with a fingertip. "Not hard enough to cut," she reported.

"That's okay," I said. "You can keep it."

"No way! You've got to get your half. I'll find a container." We looked in a cupboard full of loose Tupperware bowls and lids. Lots of them looked like they would match, but none of them quite did.

"It's okay Bridget," I said as she rummaged for the right lid. "Keep it."

"That wouldn't be fair."

"I don't mind. Really," I said, worried about the gathering darkness.

"What about a bag?"

"Whatever's quickest," I said.

Bridget was spooning the half-set fudge into a sandwich bag when I heard footsteps on the stairs. Paige was coming down.

"I've gotta go," I cried, rushing for the front door.

"But your fudge!"

"'S okay," I called from the Hanrahan's front doorstep.

"Rosie!" Bridget ran down her front walkway in stocking feet. "Here!"

She handed me the fudge. I grabbed it as though I was running a relay. "Thanks," I called as I sprinted up the sidewalk. "I'll phone you."

"Okay," Bridget said, but there was a question in her voice.

I knew I was acting weird, but I had no choice. I had to get where Paige couldn't offer me a ride. I ran, my plastic bag of fudge swinging from my fist. I turned the corner, and there was Devo. Matt, Zach and Heath were with him.

"Look. It's McGrady, out stealing dog poo," Devo said, but he used a ruder word. Then he said a bunch of things too gross to repeat. They all laughed and laughed. I should have said something sarcastic, but all I did was walk past dangling my bag.

"She is one very weird person," Devo concluded. And of course they all agreed.

NOTEBOOK: #20

NAME: Rosamund McGrady

SUBJECT: Smithereens

Darkness came even earlier in December. I therefore had to leave Bridget's even earlier to avoid a ride to my so-called home. Sometimes this got awkward. For example, the time that Bridget and I were making a gingerbread house. We were at a crucial stage: the egg-white icing was thick but not hard. With both hands I held my half of the roof and Bridget held hers. As the icing dried the December sky darkened. It was almost completely dark when the headlights of Paige's minivan swung through the family room. She was returning from the supermarket.

"Bridget, I've gotta go," I said. I pushed my chair back from the table, abandoning my construction duties.

"Don't go now," said Bridget. "Wait 'til. . . ."

"I can't!" I said at the sound of the automatic garage door.

"But I can't hold your side of the roof too! The chimney's gonna fall off if I let go! Can't you just wait until. . . ."

"I can't," I said. I heard Paige's footsteps in the mudroom, trudging toward me like doom. "I really can't. Sorry."

"But. . . ."

I grabbed my jacket. My half of the roof slid off the gingerbread eaves and broke into a half-dozen brittle pieces.

"Our roof!" Bridget yelled.

"Sorry, sorry, sorry," I said, running for her front door.

It took days to repair the damage to the gingerbread house. We made more dough, and we made more icing. Bridget didn't seem to blame me, but I worried she'd start thinking I was crazy.

Soon after the gingerbread house we made Christmas ornaments. I fled the moment we had set out all the supplies. Another afternoon, I ran off before I'd finished decorating my first gingerbread man. "I've gotta go," I cried in routine panic. My gingerbread man gave me a puzzled look with the Smartie eyes that were his only feature.

It was frustrating. I knew just how Cinderella felt, running away from a good time to stop people from finding out about her living conditions.

The last thing I wanted to do was tell any more lies, but I had to explain my habit of running off right in the middle of our fun. As an excuse for leaving early, I told Paige and Bridget that my parents had signed me up for five o'clock lessons. I thought up all kinds of subjects for my pretend lessons, like Mandarin and clarinet and highland dancing, but I worried that I would be asked to demonstrate my skills. I decided on pretend lessons in cooking.

I hated lying. I wanted what I said to be the truth, so I

started taking my five o'clock cooking lessons seriously. I taught myself. I got cookbooks from the library, and picked recipes to make for dinner. It made me feel like less of a liar, and it made my parents happy too. Late one December afternoon I was in the supermarket buying alfredo sauce when my cell phone rang. It was Mom, saying that she and Dad were staying at the university to hear some special lecture, so could I please pick Tilley up at Eveline's? I wrote the address on my hand and backtracked to Eveline's. The cold evening air tingled in my lungs.

Eveline's was a house a lot like Bridget's, not too far away. I pressed the doorbell and listened to the long complicated chime. The door opened and there, at the threshold, was Kendra. Her mouth closed and her eyes looked me up and down. As for my own face, I was staring too. I was totally surprised to see Kendra there. It had never occurred to me that Eveline was one of the Smithereens.

When Kendra and I saw each other at school each day we'd narrow our eyes and close our mouths and silently declare ourselves enemies. But I did not feel that I could behave the same way on her doorstep. "Oh, uh, hi," I said, as if it was normal for us to speak. "I'm here to pick up my sister, Tilley."

Kendra walked off. "Tilley, your *sister's* here," she yelled.

A Mrs. Smith–type person came to the front door. "Come in, come in, they're just in the family room" she said, and I had to follow her. Two boy Smithereens sat with Kendra on the family room couch, in the jumping blue light of the TV. Tilley and Eveline were standing there twining arms like they couldn't stand to part.

"Now girls, you can play again tomorrow. They are the *best* of friends," Mrs. Smith said, turning to me. "We're very fond of Tilley. She's just been telling me how you all live in a treehouse."

"Ha, ha," I said, appalled. "Tilley has a great little imagination."

Tilley turned from Eveline to look at me.

"Well, I *wondered*," Mrs. Smith said. "But my goodness, all the *details* she came up with! She made it all so *vivid*." Kendra seized the remote and turned down the TV volume.

"She always did have a great imagination," I said, and I patted Tilley's head.

Tilley ducked her head from my hand. "I do NOT have a great imagination!" she said indignantly.

"Oh, but Tilley, it's a *wonderful* thing, to have a good imagination," Mrs. Smith said.

"Yeah, Tilley," I said. "It's good you're so creative." I glanced at Kendra. She still faced the TV, but she was examining me through the back of her head. That's what it felt like anyway.

"I do NOT have a good imagination! I am NOT creative!" Tears of rage pooled in Tilley's eyes.

"Oh, but of course you do, dear, of course you are," Mrs. Smith soothed.

"Yeah, Tilley," I said. "You do. You are."

"The treehouse is real!" Tilley cried. Kendra turned to look.

"It's real to *you*, Tilley," I said. "Which is great. That's how fantabulous your imagination is."

Tilley stared at me. "Stop acting like the treehouse

isn't real!" she shouted.

I turned to Mrs. Smith. "Tilley is used to me participating in her fantasies," I said. "We try to do that, as a family." I patted Tilley's head again, but she batted my hand away.

"That's lovely," Mrs. Smith said. "The world of make-believe is so important at this age."

Eveline was looking from her mother, to Tilley, to me, trying to figure out what was going on. Tilley was quivering with fury. I had to get her out of there before she said another word. "Thank you for having her," I said. I made a grab for Tilley. She tried to avoid me, but I chased her into a corner and clamped onto her wrist.

"Tilley, what do you say?" I said.

She bent over double, trying to squirm away. "Thank. You. For. Having me," Tilley said, teeth clenched for her escape attempt.

"Nice having you, Tilley," Mrs. Smith said, but she looked a bit concerned about the struggle in her family room. "See you soon."

With Tilley more or less under arrest, I marched her out the front door and down Kendra's walkway. When I let her go she whipped around to face me. "Why did you say that we don't live in a treehouse when WE DO TOO!"

"I didn't," I said. "I never said we don't live in a treehouse. All I said was that you have a great imagination."

"LIAR!"

"It's not a lie. You do have a great imagination. Everybody says so. You should be proud of it."

Tilley squished her lips together. She opened her mouth a couple of times to speak, but didn't. She could tell there was something wrong with what I was saying but she didn't know exactly what. She thought hard, then punched me on the arm.

"Tilley!"

"You deserve it," Tilley said.

No way would I admit this to her. "Violence is never justified," I said, quoting Mom and Dad. Tilley went to punch me again, and when I grabbed her wrist she kicked my leg. "Tilley! You brat."

"*You're* the brat," she said.

"*You* are," I said.

"*You* are."

"*You* are."

"*You* are."

"*You* are."

"*You* are."

I decided not to continue this conversation into infinity. I had just seen the slightest parting of the Smith's living room curtains and I guessed that my fight with Tilley was being observed. "Let's *go*," I said, and we stalked along the sidewalk. Tilley's angry breath was like dragon smoke, pluming out of her nostrils into the cold evening air. I tried to be just as mad as she was, but somehow I couldn't do it.

At the edge of the woods we silently fished our headlamps from our backpacks and strapped them on. The moment I unlocked her bike Tilley rode furiously away, her LED light bouncing ahead on the path. When we got near the treehouse she clattered her bike into our shed and stormed the ladder up the trunk.

"Careful! It's slippery," I called as I grasped the first icy rung. Tilley did not answer.

The treehouse door had been swollen since the fall rains and Tilley couldn't open it herself. When I thumped it open she rushed into the dark treehouse and threw herself face down on her bunk. I stood there in the cold, watching her in the thin beam of my headlamp. "*Tilley*," I said. I was about to tell her that what I'd said at the Smith's wasn't such a big deal, but then I realized something. The whole reason I had made *her* best friend think that Tilley had lied about where *she* lived was so that *my* best friend wouldn't think I had lied about where *I* lived. So I couldn't exactly say it wasn't a big deal.

Face down on the mattress, Tilley shouted "I HATE YOU."

I said nothing. There wasn't much I could say.

NOTEBOOK: #21

NAME: Rosamund McGrady

SUBJECT: The Contract

Tilley lay in her bunk, facing the wall. "Tilley," I said softly into the dark, but Tilley didn't answer. As I stood watching her from the bunk ladder, I began to freeze in the unheated treehouse.

"Cold, isn't it," I said to Tilley's rigid back.

"How about I'll make us a nice fire?" Tilley's silence was cold as the air. I lit a kerosene lantern and got firewood from the porch. "Don't worry, Tilley, I'll get you all nice and warm," I said, kneeling to arrange the kindling in the cast-iron stove. With mittens still on, I struck a match and held it inside. The flame kept stubbornly to itself before catching.

"Nice fire, huh, Tilley," I said when flames finally leapt in the stove. She still didn't answer. By then I was chilled right through. I climbed to my bunk and curled fully dressed under my quilt.

After a long silence I called out. "Hey Tilley, what do

you feel like for dinner? Macaroni and cheese with bacon bits?" This was her favourite, so I thought she'd answer for sure. But I was wrong.

"Okay, mac and cheese with bacon bits coming up," I said. I got out of bed to pump water, but found the pump handle frozen into place by a coating of ice. I got a hot poker from our cast-iron stove to melt it and then I pumped for what seemed like forever. The night air was so cold it prickled the inside of my nostrils.

Tilley was sitting up in bed when I banged open the door with my pot of water. She looked me in the eye and threw herself back down on the bunk. "Getting hungry, Tilley?" I asked, setting the pot down. Water sloshed on the cast-iron stove and sizzled into nothing. Otherwise, there was silence. I was surprised by how long Tilley was keeping up her protest. I thought she'd get bored. As I fried the bacon, she flung off her quilt and I hoped this meant she was returning to normal. It didn't. The treehouse was just hot, was all, from the blaze in the cast-iron stove.

When my parents came home and we all sat down to dinner, Tilley still wouldn't talk to me. At bedtime I left the sweltering heat of the treehouse to brush my teeth on the porch. I spat a glob of toothpaste over the banister, wondering if it would freeze solid before hitting the ground. When my parents sent Tilley out to brush her teeth I found myself alone with her. "Come on, Tilley," I begged. "Please don't be mad." But when Tilley turned toward me, it was only to make a gargoyle face.

That night I lay awake in my bunk, feeling the heat of the dying fire seep away. I curled tighter and tighter to keep warm. By morning my porthole was coated inside with frost crystals. I moved a millimeter and was shocked by the cold of my sheets. As I lay there, hibernating against the terrible cold of the treehouse, I remembered how mad Tilley had been at bedtime. I hoped that maybe the night had erased her memory. But when Dad got the fire going and it was warm enough to venture from our bunks, Tilley was mad as ever.

"Do you want some hot chocolate, Tilley?" I offered.

"No," she said.

"You mean no thank you," Dad corrected.

"No *thank you*," Tilley said, but in a very ungrateful voice.

"That's not like you, Tilley," Mom said. "It'll warm you up."

"Okay," said Tilley to Mom. "If *you* make it for me."

Mom went out to pump water, but came back into the treehouse empty handed. "David," she said, "the pump won't work. Our water pipe has frozen."

"Frozen? Oh no."

"It's okay. We'll fill a few pots from the stream, that's all. The girls can do that and we'll winch them up."

Tilley and I bundled up and went out into the arctic cold. Down below we collected the pots from the dumbwaiter. I watched Tilley march toward the stream, empty pot bumping against her leg. I was worried. In the mood she was in, Tilley was dangerous. She could decide to *prove* to the Smithereens that she lived in a treehouse. She could get Mom and Dad to be her witnesses. She could bring the Smithereens to our home. She could show treehouse pictures from our photo CD. The evidence existed. I had to convince Tilley not to use it.

I came to an awful conclusion. There was only one

way out of this situation. It was a drastic, desperate solution. I was going to have to apologize.

I caught up to Tilley when she paused to smash an ice puddle. "Tilley," I said, but she marched onward. I caught up to her again at the stream. Ice was forming at the bank. I opened my mouth to deliver the apology, but nothing came out but a big winter cloud of breath. The apology was stuck in my throat, like a whole piece of popcorn. I tried again and managed to get it out. "Tilley. I'm sorry," I said, sounding like I was reading from a card. "You were right that I was lying to Mrs. Smith. I did it because Bridget thinks we live in Grand Oak Manor and I didn't want Kendra telling her that we just live in a treehouse. I'm sorry. I mean it. I am."

The apology worked instantly. "Okay," Tilley said. "How come Bridget thinks you live in Grand Oak Manor?"

"Accident. She thought it by mistake and I didn't explain in time. I wish I had."

"So, you're gonna tell Bridget about the treehouse now?" Tilley asked.

"Well, no," I said. "I'm not."

"You just said you wished you'd told Bridget," Tilley pointed out.

"I *do* wish I had," I said. "But that's not the same as wanting to tell her *now*."

"It's not?" asked Tilley.

"No."

"I don't get why not."

"Well, it's hard to explain."

"So you're just gonna tell Mrs. Smith and Eveline?" Tilley asked.

"No," I said. "Then Bridget would find out."

"You just said you were sorry you lied to Mrs. Smith." Tilley's frown was coming back.

"I am."

"Then how come you want to keep doing it?" Tilley asked.

"It's not that I *want* to," I said. "I *need* to. And I need you to help me."

"Help you lie?"

"Well," I said. "Yeah."

"Uh uh," Tilley shook her head like she was trying to get a bug out of her hair. "I only tell Eveline true stuff."

I knelt with my pot, letting the stream water flow into it. I lugged it to the dumbwaiter, still thinking. As the dumbwaiter rose toward the treehouse, Tilley and her pot sloshed toward me. "Tilley," I said. "Would Eveline keep a secret if you asked her?"

"Yuh!" said Tilley, putting her pot down. "'Cause she's my best friend."

"Then listen," I said. "How about *I'll* tell Eveline the treehouse is real if you and Eveline both promise that *you'll* pretend to Mrs. Smith and Kendra and everybody else that the treehouse is just pretend?"

"Pretend it's pretend?" Tilley asked.

"Yeah. And if you do it, I'll be so, so, so nice to you," I promised. "Really, really nice."

"How about Eveline?"

"I'll be really nice to her too," I said. "Really really. Any way she can think up."

"Okay," Tilley said. "Then I promise."

I breathed a big wintry cloud of relief.

The dumbwaiter dropped. We put Tilley's pot in, then climbed to the treehouse and got ready for school. It was too cold to ride our bikes. As Tilley and I walked down the path of frosted branches, I asked whether Mrs. Smith had ever talked about the treehouse with Mom and Dad when they'd picked her up. No, Tilley said. Maybe Mrs. Smith didn't believe we lived in a treehouse, I thought, or maybe she thought living in a treehouse was a big embarrassment for grownups. Who knew? The important thing was that she'd never talked about the treehouse with Mom and Dad. This meant that the Smithereens and Kendra had never heard about the treehouse from anybody truly believable. It meant that none of them would know the treehouse was real if Eveline would co-operate.

When we got to the grounds of Sir Combover I was glad to see Eveline already there in her little pink jacket with the fuzzy bunny pockets. "Go talk to her," I said. Tilley ran over to Eveline and they talked for ages as I stood with the cold of the asphalt seeping into my boots. Finally they came over. "Eveline agrees," Tilley said. "But she wants a contract."

"A contract?" I thought this was cute. "Saying what?"

Tilley looked at Eveline. "About the being nice," Eveline said.

"Okay," I said, because I wanted Eveline to like the idea. I rummaged in my backpack for writing paper. I found a crumpled math test, blank on one side. To make up for the messy paper I used fancy language, which was easy for me because Miss Rankle had spent about seven hours on contracts in personal skills. I balanced my wobbling math textbook on my knee, and wrote in the best handwriting I could manage with mitts on. To embellish the contract, I added lots of curlicues. Then I read the whole thing out loud.

In consideration for not revealing the existence<br>of the McGrady residential treehouse,<br>I, Rosamund McGrady, do hereby undertake<br>to be nice to Matilda McGrady and Eveline Smith<br>in such ways as they may specify.

I wrote the date and signed with a flourish. Tilley and Eveline signed too, in great big crooked block letters that took up the rest of the page. Each party to a contract is supposed to get a copy, but I'd be late for school if I wrote it out in triplicate. Eveline was really the only one who wanted it, so I just gave it to her. Of course she couldn't read it, but she looked all happy before she folded it into her bunny pocket. She gave me a big gap-toothed Grade One smile, and I went off to Windward with the cozy feeling that my secret was safe.

| | |
|---|---|
| NOTEBOOK: | #22 |
| NAME: | Rosamund McGrady |
| SUBJECT: | Footprints |

The Windward students were very privileged. You could say they were spoiled. This was especially clear in December, when they started talking about holiday plans. Just about everybody was going to Mexico or Hawaii or Florida. The Smithereens were going to southern Italy for a month: Kendra broadcast this in a voice meant for the whole classroom. Devo did some high-volume bragging too, about renting a twelfth-century palace on a privately owned island off the north coast of Morocco. I couldn't help feeling jealous. It all sounded so warm, and the treehouse was getting so cold.

Once Eveline left for southern Italy, Tilley had nowhere to go after school except home to the treehouse. This meant that I had to go with her. Treehouse life was hard at that time. The water pipe was still frozen solid. All our water was scooped right from the stream and hauled up to the treehouse in the dumbwaiter. Water is amazingly heavy, and the average North American uses 343 litres per day, so using the dumbwaiter for our water supply was literally tons of work.

"I don't know, Andrea," Dad said one evening as he staggered into the treehouse with a big pot. He had just winched up the daily water supply. "The treehouse has been great, but we can't keep on doing this."

"But think of all the people in the world who have to travel to their water supplies," Mom said. She set the pot on the stove to boil any parasites dead. "For miles, some of them. *They* keep on doing it."

"Because they have no choice," Dad said. "We do."

"The choice of some depressing apartment?" Mom asked. "Oh David, no. The pipe won't stay frozen forever."

"It's December," Dad said. "We've got at least two more months of winter."

"But winter isn't usually as cold as this. This is unusual," Mom said.

"We should have insulated the pipe."

"So let's insulate it now."

"I'm not sure we should sink any more money into this place Andrea. I always said it wasn't practical."

Despite the hardship of winter, Tilley and I were terrified at the suggestion of moving from the treehouse. We therefore helped draw water without complaint. As soon as we got home, Tilley would fill the pots in the stream and I would winch them up. Then I'd winch up lots of firewood, because the treehouse was literally freezing cold inside. Mom and Dad's leftover morning coffee was ice; the washing-up water in our porcelain pitcher was ice. The inside of our propane fridge was the warmest place in the treehouse. I'd make a fire first thing after school, then Tilley and I would hop into our bunks, still wearing toques and jackets and mitts. We'd watch the firelight glow on the polished wooden walls as we waited for the treehouse to heat. Luckily, the treehouse heated fast. Pretty soon we'd peel off our outdoor clothes, and throw back our quilts, and emerge into the new coziness. I would do my homework by lantern light, and Tilley would cut fancy snowflakes and tape them to the treehouse windows. I lent her my special bird scissors, which made ultra-precise cuts now that Dad had tightened up the screw. Tilley was passionate about her snowflakes. It got so you could hardly see outside except through the cut-outs.

"Let's make the whole treehouse Christmassy," Tilley said, so one afternoon we went out and gathered holly from the grounds to make a wreath. Making a wreath out of holly was not easy. It felt like being attacked by a small vicious animal, but the wreath looked good. The bloodstains were not obvious.

Another afternoon we scavenged fallen pine and fir boughs from the grounds, and festooned them around the treehouse ceiling. We added red berry clusters for colour. The boughs smelled like the essence of Christmas, and for awhile Tilley and I lay on my bunk, inhaling as hard as we could. "You know that the supermarket sells boughs just like these ones," I told Tilley. "We saved major mega-bucks by getting them from the woods." Before I'd finished this sentence an idea had formed.

That Saturday, Tilley and I gathered more boughs and loaded them into the bike trailer. We rode through the frosted woods to the supermarket, wearing so many layers that it was hard to bend our legs to pedal. In the corner of the supermarket parking lot I brought out my cardboard sign and placed it on the trailer. *BOUGHS FOR SALE*, it said. The sign had looked okay when I'd been lettering it at our folding table, but out in the harsher atmosphere of a public place it suddenly looked unprofessional. I thought that Tilley, being cute, would attract customers, but we stood around a long time in that freezing parking lot, totally ignored. It seems weird that being ignored would make a person feel conspicuous, but that's how I felt. I worried about being seen. I kept making false sightings of Devo and Sienna and Twyla in the parking cars. I was feeling like a loser and was thinking about giving up and going home when we got our first customer, a nice lady who bought four bundles. Customers seem to attract more customers, and then business was brisk. My zippered plastic bag filled up with bills and coins. After awhile there was so much that I didn't even have to ask people for exact change. Tilley and I stayed until the last boughs were sold.

"I think I've got frostbite," I said.

"What's frostbite?"

"When your body can't heat your nose and fingers and toes because it's saving the heat for your insides," I said.

"I have that," Tilley said.

"And I think I've got hypothermia too," I said.

"What's that?"

"When your body can't heat your insides either."

"I totally have that for sure," Tilley said.

"The cure is hot chocolate. Let's go home," I said, and we rode off, the empty bike trailer bumping along behind us. I had just come through the trap door onto the treehouse porch when I saw a snowflake pirouette from the blank grey sky. "It's snowing," I yelled, and by the time Tilley reached the porch the air twirled with flakes. We hung over the porch, monitoring the meadow below us to see whether the snow would stick. It did. It stuck, and filled in, and piled up, and hurried from the sky. It kept on snowing at bedtime. I slept with my porthole window open, staring into the blizzard until I got optical illusions. Every now and then a snowflake would stray through the porthole and melt on my cheek, and I'd snap back to my ordinary senses.

The next morning the treehouse was bright with snowlight. Through Tilley's paper snowflakes we could see the oak branches doubled in snow. Tilley and I hurried to get ready. We had already decided that this was our Christmas-shopping day. Mom and Dad were still drinking morning coffee when Tilley and I climbed the ladder down the trunk, keen to make the first tracks across the smooth white meadow. But as we descended, we saw that we were too late.

"Hey," Tilley said. "Something came here." There were tracks leading right up to the giant oak.

"*Somebody* came here," I said as I reached the bottom of the ladder. The tracks were footprints. They came from the gate in the so-called electric fence, and returned there as well. "Great-great-aunt Lydia came here. Weird. I wonder why."

"Maybe she likes making footprints in new snow too," Tilley suggested.

"Somehow I don't think that's it." As I stepped into the snow, I saw something on the oak trunk. It was a blue envelope, thumbtacked to the bark. "The McGradys," the envelope said. The handwriting was familiar: fancy but shaky.

"Tilley," I said. "Great-great-aunt Lydia has written us a letter." I removed the thumbtack as carefully as if I were gathering evidence at a crime scene. I handled the envelope by its corners. I held it for a long time, to prolong the excitement of finding out what Great-great-aunt Lydia had to say. Finally I untucked the paper flap and opened the envelope.

"What the . . ." I said. "It's empty!"

"Empty?"

I shook the envelope upside down. "Empty," I confirmed. "So why did Great-great-aunt Lydia trudge all the way over here in two feet of snow just to leave us an empty envelope? She is *so* weird."

"Yeah," said Tilley. "Weird." I tucked the envelope into my jacket pocket.

There was way too much snow for bike riding. Tilley and I waded through the lacy white tunnel of woods until we reached the sidewalk. We caught the bus, taking the bus fare from our plastic bag of bough money. The bus seemed an exotic form of travel. The destination was exotic too, at least to us. We were going to the mall.

Upon arrival, we ran up the down escalator and down the up escalator a few times to satisfy Tilley's urges. Then we wandered through the stores, humming mall carols and picking presents. Out of the bough money, Tilley bought Eveline a spy kit with a periscope. I bought Bridget a really cool friendship bracelet, made of braided cord and silver beads.

On the way out of the mall we saw Santa Claus sitting on his throne. Since she's only six, Tilley got all excited and we joined the line of waiting kids. When it was our turn, Tilley sat on one red velveteen knee and I sat on the other.

"Ho, ho, ho," Santa said. "And what are your names?"

"Tilley," said Tilley.

"Rosie," I said.

We told him what we wanted for Christmas and, presto, we had two free candy canes.

"Hey," I said, as we followed the red velvet ropes to the exit from Santa's Castle. "These would look really good on the boughs in the treehouse." I looked over my shoulder at Santa. Clearly, he was a valuable resource. Tilley and I went straight back to the end of the line-up, taking off our jackets and toques to change our appearance. When we reached Santa for the second time we introduced ourselves as Matilda and Rosamund. We made a third trip as Matty and Rosa, this time with our hair pulled back into elastic bands that I'd found in my pocket. On our fourth trip we stuck out our teeth and called ourselves Tilda and Mundie. On the fifth trip we puffed out our cheeks with air and used our middle names, Penelope and Millicent.

By this time I'd memorized all the veins in Santa's nose, so I was really not surprised when he recognized us. "Ho, ho, ho," he said. "You girls certainly do like visiting with old Santa Claus."

"It's the candy canes," Tilley admitted. "We want them for decorations." Santa gave us three candy canes each that visit, which was very nice of him, considering that we'd already sort of abused his hospitality.

We left the mall and crossed the street to Home Depot. "Excuse me," I said to a salesman in a zippered orange shirt. "I need insulation for an exterior water pipe."

"Why do you need insulation for an exterior water pipe?" he asked. He sounded very guarded. I think he thought my request for insulation was some kind of in-person prank call, and that all of my Grade Seven friends were hiding on the shelves behind the microwave boxes, giggling at him.

"My parents need it," I explained. "It's my Christmas present to them."

"You're buying insulation as a Christmas present." He said it skeptically, to show that he was no fool.

"Yes," I said, and I described what I needed. I wasn't sure he believed me, but twenty minutes later I had a cart full of self-adhesive foam pipe insulation, cut in six foot lengths. I was a bit daunted by the mass of it. As I fished the cash from my plastic bag, I wondered how Tilley and I were going to get it home on the bus.

"Rosie," I heard. I looked up to see Paige, one lineup over.

"Oh, Paige, hi," I said. "You've met my little sister, Tilley."

"Yes, on Halloween. Hi Tilley. Now Rosie, what is that in your cart?"

"In my cart? Oh, this. This is pipe insulation."

"What on earth are you doing buying insulation?"

"Umm. It's for the renovation."

"For the renovation? But why are you girls the ones out buying it?"

"Why are we the ones? Oh. Umm. Our contractor just asked us to pick it up, that's all."

"Your contractor asked you and your little sister to go buy the insulation?" Paige looked astounded. "Who is your contractor?"

"Our contractor?"

"Yes. Your contractor. This is so unusual! Who is it?"

Once again, pressure had pressed everything from my mind. As I stood there at the check-out, my mind contained not a single thing, except what was before my eyes. "Gum and mints," I said. "And company."

"Gummen Minz and Company," Paige repeated. "I don't know them. How on earth are you girls going to get this home? Can I give you a lift?"

"Oh no. No. Our Dad is picking us up. In his car. Yeah. He's out on the parking lot. In his car. Right now. We're just watching his cart."

"Oh, good. Well, that makes a *bit* more sense then. Okay, bye now girls. See you soon."

The cashier put the insulation into three huge plastic bags that Tilley and I dragged like sleds over the snow to the bus stop. When the bus came we couldn't get the bags up the steps until passengers jumped out of the courtesy seats to help. It was extremely tiring dragging those huge bags down the long, snowy path through the woods, but I was glad to do it. I would have done just about anything to keep on living in the treehouse.

NOTEBOOK: #23

NAME: Rosamund McGrady

SUBJECT: Blackmail

On the last school day in December, Miss Rankle commanded our class to recite "The Night Before Christmas" at the Volunteer Tea. Only Kendra, who was already in Italy, escaped this embarrassment. When our class got to the 'breast of the new-fallen snow' there was a lot of immaturity by Devo and his friends. Miss Rankle made us all stay afterward for a scalding lecture. But finally she finished with us and we were on Christmas holiday.

I couldn't go over to Bridget's because I had to pick up Tilley. Since Bridget was leaving for Hawaii the next day, she walked with me to Sir Combover. Outside the school grounds she handed me a small square box. The one I handed her was the exact same size. When we unwrapped them we laughed. We'd given identical bracelets.

"Coincidence?" I said.

"I think not," said Bridget.

"No. It's great minds thinking alike."

"It's karma." We put the bracelets on, and I felt that we were now officially best friends.

Christmas Day sparkled with snow. Tilley and I got new clothes, which pleased me more than her. My parents were thrilled with the self-adhesive foam pipe insulation. They applied it as soon as we'd finished Christmas breakfast.

Post-Christmas has never been my favourite time of year, and the treehouse didn't change my mind. Mom and Dad were off from university, and we'd planned to spend the holidays frolicking in the winter wonderland of Great-great-aunt Lydia's woods, but that's not what happened. Right after Christmas it warmed up. Snow mush fell past our windows and water flowed in the pipe again. It was too wet to play outside, so we didn't. Then the temperature dropped back below freezing. With its new insulation the pipe was fine, but the melting snow froze solid. The rungs of the treehouse ladder were so deadly slippery, that Dad rented a mountaineer's ropes and harness, plus spiked crampons for our boots. The novelty of the mountaineering equipment wore off fast. It was a huge nuisance to get to and from the treehouse. Mom and Dad kept sending Tilley and me out to play anyway, and we hated it. There was nothing to do when we reached the ground. It was no fun clumping along in crampons, and even down there it was hazardous without them. Mom and Dad looked fed up when Tilley and I kept reappearing in the treehouse doorway. I could see why. The treehouse was not designed for four unoccupied people. It got on my nerves too, that wherever I looked or stepped, there everybody was. We all got really crabby, and we were all glad to go back to school.

It was great to see Bridget again, all tanned from Hawaii. Kendra was back from Italy, air-kissing her friends and saying "ciao" to everybody except me and Bridget. She kept staring at our matching bracelets.

Eveline was back, too, and when the first day of school ended Tilley called my cell to say she was going to her house. "Okay," I said. I had basically forgotten my promise to be nice to Tilley and Eveline in return for keeping quiet about the treehouse. Tilley seemed to have forgotten too: she hadn't mentioned it once in the three and a half weeks since the promise. I would have thought that Eveline was the most likely of all three of us to forget about it. After all, she was the one who had been away in Italy being all distracted with foreign words, and different food, and statues of naked people. But I thought wrong. Eveline remembered.

When I took Tilley to Sir Combover Elementary the next morning, Eveline was waiting, looking cute as ever. She cupped both hands around Tilley's ear, and whispered for a long time. She didn't whisper as loud as most little kids, so I had no clue what was going on. Tilley looked kind of worried. She whispered back for a second, then Eveline lunged for her ear again and whispered some more. Finally, Eveline stepped back.

"Umm," Tilley said. She stood making clouds of breath. Eveline jiggled Tilley's elbow.

"Umm. Like. You promised to be nice to us?" Tilley stopped and Eveline whispered at her. Tilley started again. "In ways as we may spe-fi-cy. Is what you said. In that contract thingy?" Tilley stopped and looked up at me.

"Yeah?" I said. "And?"

Tilley bit her lip until Eveline whispered at her again. "So the way we speficy is, we want toffee,"Tilley concluded. "MacIntosh's Creamy Toffee."

"And you want me to buy it?" I asked.

Tilley opened her mouth but said nothing. Eveline nodded.

"You do," I said. "Yeah. Well. Okay, I guess." It was perfectly natural for little kids to want toffee, I told myself as I headed off to Windward. Still, I had a bad feeling.

The bough money was all gone, and my allowance was very small. Measured in MacIntosh's Creamy Toffee, it was two boxes worth, so buying a box for Eveline and Tilley meant giving up half my treat money for the week. I did it because I *had* promised to be nice to them in such ways as they might specify, but I hoped it wouldn't happen again.

It did happen again, two days later, on allowance day. It was the same as before. Eveline hissed in Tilley's ear, and Tilley was the spokesperson.

"Umm,"Tilley said. "That toffee? We finished it? And, like. We. Want some more."

Eveline jiggled Tilley's elbow. "A box each," Tilley added.

"A box each! Tilley, that's my whole allowance!"

Tilley looked at Eveline, to see what she thought of my protest. They whispered to each other until Eveline nudged Tilley forward. Tilley opened her mouth. "Eveline says one box for two people isn't enough."

"That's not fair," I said.

Like a snake striking, Eveline went for Tilley's ear.

"Eveline says you promised, so it is fair, Eveline says," said Tilley.

I stared down at Eveline's Hello Kitty barrettes. "Fine!" I said, twirling myself off toward Windward.

On Monday morning at Sir Combover Elementary there was another demand for MacIntosh's Creamy Toffee.

"I can't get anymore," I said. "I've spent my allowance for this week. The whole thing. Remember?"

They whispered.

"Eveline has money you can use," Tilley said.

"Then why doesn't she just buy it herself?"

"Grade Ones aren't allowed to go to the store by themselves," Tilley said.

"So why doesn't she go with her mom?"

"Her mom won't let her buy it," Tilley said. "She says it rots her teeth. Same as our mom."

Eveline gave some change to Tilley, who handed it on to me. When I delivered the toffee at Sir Combover the next morning, Eveline was already digging quarters from her fuzzy bunny pocket, and Tilley was already asking for more.

"Your teeth *are* going to rot," I said.

Eveline whispered. "Eveline says that's none of your business," Tilley said. More whispering. "Eveline says you promised to be nice, and she says we get to decide what's nice, and we think toffee is nice," Tilley reported.

I got the toffee, but I was starting to feel like a drug dealer, supplying kids with all this unhealthy stuff. On Thursday, Eveline and Tilley made a new demand.

"Eveline wants you to take us to Lester's Pizza Hideaway," Tilley said. "At lunchtime tomorrow."

"I can't take you for lunch! That's way more than my allowance."

"Eveline says she has enough money,"Tilley said.

"How does Eveline have all this money?" I asked.

"She gets it off her mother's dresser,"Tilley said, and Eveline elbowed her.

I opened my mouth to act shocked. And even though I easily could have kept my mouth closed, I actually *was* kind of shocked. The angelic-looking Eveline, I was starting to think, had the makings of a young offender. "I still can't," I said. "You need a note from your parents to leave the school grounds at lunch."

Eveline whispered. "Eveline says you can do the notes because you know all the big words and how to spell them and everything,"Tilley said.

"You want me to *forge* a permission note?" I demanded.

Tilley looked at Eveline to see if this really *was* what they wanted. Eveline narrowed her big blue eyes and nodded.

"That's dishonest," I said. "Forget it."

From her fuzzy bunny pocket Eveline brought out a paper and unfolded it. I made a grab but she balled it up in her fist. It was the old math test that I'd used for the contract. In a flash, I'd seen my printed name and Miss Rankle's red-pen comments. I suddenly realized that I had supplied Eveline with positive proof of the exact fact I was trying to keep secret. She tucked her evidence back inside her bunny pocket.

"Okay," I said. I was nearly as mad at my own stupidity as I was at them.

"My mom's name is Jocelyn," Eveline said, and I was startled to hear her speak out loud. She handed me a cancelled cheque with her mother's signature. I shoved it in my pencil case.

That afternoon I practiced forgery on the folding table in the treehouse. I signed the names Jocelyn Smith and Andrea McGrady fifty times each, then burnt these practice signatures in the cast-iron stove. Under the cover of my math textbook I hid the two good-copy forgeries. I tossed in my berth that night, staring out my porthole at the bare oak branches all coated in moonlight. It bugged me that I was about to commit a semi-criminal act. Next morning, I glared at Tilley at breakfast and I said nothing as I walked her through the woods to Sir Combover Elementary. My only pleasure was in ignoring all her tries at talking to me.

At Sir Combover I handed the forgeries over to Tilley and Eveline. I came back at lunchtime and wordlessly led them to Lester's Pizza Hideaway. Tilley dropped a handful of coins into my hand, and with this stolen property I paid for their food. I brought the paper plates to their table and put them down so hard that the pizza slices leapt in terror. I slammed myself into my own plastic chair. Tilley looked at me nervously and started a conference of whispering. Finally, Tilley spoke. "Eveline has money for you to buy pizza too," she said.

"No thank you," I said. "I don't want to live off the proceeds of crime. Unlike some." I opened my lunch bag, but before my second bite of smoked oyster sandwich the pizza guy told me that bagged lunches weren't allowed. I put my sandwich away and sat starving, while Tilley and Eveline ate. I scowled. My strategy was to be so grumpy that they would have no fun at all and would be sorry that they came. Tilley did look uncomfortable, but not Eveline. I think she was totally used to making people grumpy.

When they'd finished I took them back to Sir

Combover. On my way back to Windward I pulled out my lunch bag, but a smoked oyster sandwich is hard to eat while walking. The oysters fell out.

Bridget had soccer and Eveline had a dentist appointment that afternoon, so Tilley and I ended up walking home together. "We did paper maché in art today," Tilley said. Silence from me, except for hard steps on old snow. "I got every single question right on my spelling test," she said. Again I said nothing. "We might go on a field trip to a space museum," she said. She sounded timid, but I didn't feel one tiny bit sorry for her. I wouldn't speak. "I think I'm getting a stomach ache," she ventured.

"All the pizza and toffee," I said. "Serves you right."

"You don't have to be so mean," Tilley said.

"No? But it's fine for you?"

"*I'm* not being mean," Tilley said.

"Oh, please."

"How am I being mean?" she asked.

"How are you being mean?" I asked. "Well now, let me think. You whisper right in front of me all the time, which is totally rude. You extort every cent of my allowance. You make me forge Mom's signature. You blackmail me."

"What's extort?" Tilley asked.

"Ask your little criminal friend. She should know."

"She is not a criminal!"

"She will be. And you will be too, if you keep on thinking you have to do every single thing she says."

"I do NOT think I have to do what she says," Tilley said.

"Well, if these are your own ideas, it's even worse. You'll be in a detention centre by the time you're twelve," I said.

"What's a tension centre?"

"It's a kiddy jail, for people like you and Eveline."

"We DO NOT deserve to go to JAIL,"Tilley cried.

"Who do you think *does* go to jail, Tilley? Dishonest people, that's who."

"Like you're so honest!"Tilley yelled. Tears dribbled. "You pretend to live in a mansion!"

"Well at least I don't steal. At least I'm not a thief like your little juvenile delinquent friend."

"Eveline is not a—what you just said. Eveline is really, really nice."

"Yeah, if you like evil people," I said.

"You're evil,"Tilley said.

"*You* are."

"*You* are."

"*You* are."

"*You* are." Tilley stomped off ahead of me, smashing through the old crusts of dirty snow.

NOTEBOOK: #24

NAME: Rosamund McGrady

SUBJECT: Panther-Lamp Day

I was really mad that Tilley was blackmailing me. Tilley was really mad that I called her and Eveline criminals. And we both stayed that way. We started avoiding eye contact, which is hard when you live in a ten-foot-square treehouse.

Like most people, Tilley wasn't very nice when she was mad. She and Eveline demanded more and more toffee and pizza lunches. They started demanding other things too, like lunchtime trips to the penny candy store, and to the video arcade, and to McDonalds. The more they blackmailed, the madder I got; and the madder I got the more I insulted Eveline; and the more I insulted Eveline the madder Tilley got; and the madder Tilley got the more she blackmailed me; and the more she blackmailed me the madder I got. Et cetera.

Near the end of January, Tilley started making demands of her own, without Eveline even there to egg her on. One Tuesday afternoon after school, I started making dinner. By then, I had a routine: Monday was supermarket-deli chicken with boiled potatoes and pre-peeled carrots with dip; Tuesday was fried leftover potatoes, fried Italian sausages and Brussels sprouts; Wednesday was sliced left-over sausages with baked beans and pre-shredded coleslaw; Thursday was some kind of pasta with salad-in-a-bag. I was getting Tuesday's Brussels sprouts and sausages and leftover potatoes out of our propane fridge when Tilley stuck her head under her bunk curtain.

"I hate Brussels sprouts," she declared.

"You love them. They're Barbie cabbages, remember?"

"To look at. Not to eat. And they stink up the whole treehouse. And those sausages are yucky, the way they ooze. I hate them too."

"Well tough luck for you," I said.

"No, tough luck for *you*. Cause I want special pasta like at Eveline's."

"You're assuming I care what you want."

"You have to care what I want."

"Says who?"

"Says me. It's what I speficy."

I stared up at Tilley in the middle bunk. A gang of Beanie Babies surrounded her, backing up her threat. And a threat is what it was.

"What is *this*, Rosie?" Mom asked at dinner that night as she lifted her first forkful of pasta.

"Spaghetti with ketchup and creamed corn," I answered. "Tilley wanted it."

"And canned beets," Mom said. "I thought you hated beets."

"Tilley likes them," I said.

A few days later after school, Tilley "speficied" that I play Barbies with her. "Okay, pretend my Barbie is visiting your Barbie in Paris," she said. "Pretend my Barbie's Canadian and your Barbie's French. Pretend the table leg is the Eiffel Tower. Okay, go."

I bobbed my blonde Barbie along the treehouse floor toward Tilley's blonde Barbie. "Excusez moi, Barbie," I said, "but my 'uge bozoms, zey is making me fall over my tres petite little feet. I zink you must alzo have zee zame problem? Vous et moi, we are zo zimilar. C'est incroyable!"

"You're not playing right," Tilley frowned. "I speficy, play properly. You say, 'Welcome to Paris, Barbie, I hope you enjoy your trip.'"

I rolled my eyes and said it.

"Do it with the accent."

I did the accent in a monotone. After that I used a monotone for all the Barbie lines that Tilley dictated. I was trying to make the game as boring for her as it was for me. Tilley wanted to keep on playing anyway, probably just to prove that she could make me.

"Playing Barbies, Rosie?" Dad asked when he came in from chopping firewood.

"Tilley wanted to play," I said.

One Saturday morning, Tilley put down her Cheerios spoon and looked across the folding table at me. "Remember that time you and me took the bus to the mall? Wasn't that fun," she asked. It was not her usual blackmail voice.

"You and me? Fun? Yeah, right. If you say so," I said. It had been fun though, and I started feeling sad.

"I want to do that again," Tilley said.

"What, are you *specifying* for me to take you to the mall?" I didn't think that this was what Tilley meant, but I needed her to say so. My voice sounded kind of mad, from habit.

Tilley looked up at me and opened her mouth. "I guess," she said finally.

"What, with Eveline?" I waited for Tilley to say no, just the two of us.

Tilley searched my face and shrugged.

"So you *do* want to go with Eveline."

Tilley shrugged again. She didn't say no.

"Why," I said, "have you been recruited into her shoplifting ring?"

Tilley jumped out of her chair and backed away from her Cheerios. "Eveline does not shoplift! Eveline would never—she would never—"

"Steal? Except from family victims?"

"Shut up! Stop acting like Eveline's a criminal!"

"Okay, Tilley. I will. As soon as Eveline stops acting like Eveline's a criminal."

"You're stupid!" Tilley yelled, charging up the ladder to her bunk.

"Lame comeback. But never mind, Tilley, your brain will continue to develop as you mature."

"I hate you," Tilley yelled, snatching up her Beanie Babies. Zip and Twigs, normally so gentle and plush, attacked each other viciously. "You know what," Tilley said a few minutes later, hanging over the side of her bunk at me. "I like the *top* bunk. I like it better than the middle."

"What are you talking about?" I said. "You hate the top.

You're scared to sleep that far from Mom and Dad. Remember?"

"That was when I was little," Tilley said. "I like the top better now. That's what I *specify*." And she was serious. I spent that Saturday morning moving my clothes and stuff down the bunk ladder. When my parents got home they found me in the middle bunk. Tilley was on top.

"Girls!" Mom said. "What's happened to your bunks?"

"Tilley wanted to switch," I said.

"Oh, Rosie," Mom said. She kissed the top of my head, and straightened up all dewy-eyed. "That is so sweet. You know, Dad and I have really noticed how considerate you've been to Tilley lately. I'm proud of how well you treat your little sister." It was weird to hear this just as I was thinking, for the first time in my life, that I really couldn't stand her. I just did not want to be around Tilley anymore. Every time she liked anything, it turned into a demand to give it to her, or buy it for her, or do it for her. I twitched whenever she opened her mouth, wondering what I'd have to do next.

I spent as little time as I could with Tilley, and as much time as I could with Bridget. It was February by then, and the days had gotten longer. At five p.m. the sky was still blue behind the bare silhouette branches. I could stay later.

Bridget and I were still working on Great-great-aunt Lydia's coded letter. We'd decided that it wasn't written in ancient English after all, since most of the words weren't in the dictionary. We started checking other languages. We thought 'LE TUSESCA PE' and 'LE TUSELO PE' might be Italian or Spanish or Latin, but they weren't. Paige was getting interested too. "Could this be Finnish?" she'd say. "Could this be Turkish?"

I was very comfortable with Paige, except when she asked how the renovations were coming. "Slowly," I would always say.

Paige would nod sympathetically. "Yup," she'd say. "That's how renovations are all right."

Sometimes I'd give Paige details, to make my reno alibi more realistic. The details were from a library book called *Avoiding Renovation Hazards*. "The contractors have just started the hazardous process of removing the urea formaldehyde foam insulation," I said once. Another time I said, "The workmen are about to apply the highly toxic floor finish." I didn't sound normal to myself when I said these things. I reminded myself of those books we have at school, where the kids say things like, "Oh Father, what a splendid day for a seaside picnic!" Paige did not seem to notice though.

"Well, I'm sure your renovation will be fabulous once it's all finished," she said one February afternoon. "All us Windward mothers are desperate for a peek. We're just dying for Panther-Lamp Day."

"Panther-Lamp Day?" I asked. "What's that?"

"Panther-Lamp Day?" Paige looked at me with disbelief. "Hasn't anybody told you about Panther-Lamp Day? Bridget, I can't believe you haven't told Rosie about Panther-Lamp Day!"

"I must have told you about Panther-Lamp Day!" Bridget said. "Panther-Lamp Day is fantastic. It rates right up there with, like, *Halloween*."

"Well, what is it?" I asked.

"It's Windward's big fundraiser," Paige said. "It's this

huge rotating rummage sale. I think somebody sold a lamp in the shape of a panther at the first one. It's the second Saturday in May every year."

"What's a rotating rummage sale?" I asked.

"Every family with kids at Windward has a rummage sale at their house," Paige said. "Somebody has to stay home to host their own sale, but the rest of the family shops at everybody else's. Actually, not *everybody* else's. Too many houses for that. Everybody picks maybe a dozen that they really want to go to."

"And I know which houses sell the good stuff," Bridget said. "You would *not* believe what some people get rid of! For cheap too! And I hate to say it, but Devo's is definitely the best for that. Some houses hold bake sales instead. Like the Wongs. Their strawberries dipped in fudge are amazing."

"Now me, I'm into household things," Paige said. "Devon's is a great house for that, because the Radcliffes redecorate a lot. And I always pick a few houses just to snoop around in. Panther-Lamp Day is definitely part home tour. I can tell you that *your* house is going to be a very popular stop, Rosie."

"It is?" I asked.

"Oh sure," Paige said.

"But," I said. "I don't know if we're participating. I don't know if the renovations will be finished by then."

"Oh *everyone* participates," Paige said. "And your reno will *definitely* be finished by then. I know renos are slow, but they don't go on forever. And if you've reached the floor finishing stage, you're almost done. Grand Oak Manor will be all back in order by Panther-Lamp Day, don't you worry."

Needless to say, I did worry. How could I not? I had no stuff to sell. I had no house to sell it from. Least of all did I have the mansion that all the Windward mothers were dying to see. I was doomed to be exposed, on Panther-Lamp Day, for the liar that I was. Kendra and Devo would never let me forget it. But it was Bridget finding out that I really feared. It scared me so much that it was all I could think of around her.

I was so zoned out with dread that I was hardly any help in trying to solve Great-great-aunt Lydia's coded letter. Then one afternoon as we lay on Bridget's family room carpet eating peanut butter cookies, she reared up. "Omigosh!" she said. "Rosie, I get it! I can't believe it took us so long to see it! These are English words, and they're in the proper order too. They're just broken up in different places! 'ID ID NO TE' is 'I did not'. And 'E' starts a new word." Bridget grabbed a pencil and started putting brackets around words. In twenty minutes we had the note solved.

(I)(D ID) (NO T)(E VER)(THIN K)(A)(PA IR)(OF)(SCIS SORS)(CO ULD)(DO) (SO)(MU CH)(HARM). (I)(HA VE)(TO)(LE AVE)(TH IS)(BLO ODY)(HO USE). (A)(BAD)(DES TIN Y)(AWA ITS) (ME)(HERE).

(A)(LI FE)(IS)(SO)(E ASI LY)(L OST).

(LE T)(US)(ESCA PE). (LE T)(US)(ELO PE).

(I SOB EL)(ME ET)(ME): (THE)(TRE EHO US E)(AT)(TEN).

X

"The letter is to someone called Isobel," Bridget said.

"That was my Great-grandmother's name," I said. "She married my Great-grampa Tavish."

"And this is him asking her to elope," Bridget said. "Wow! *He* was the one who wrote the letter, *not* your Great-great-aunt Lydia."

"So the 'X' where the signature goes, that's a kiss."

"But why is his letter on your Great-great-aunt Lydia's stationery?"

"Maybe it was handy and he was in a hurry? He sounds urgent."

"No kidding. Huge drama. The having to leave and the blood and all. What's *that* all about?"

"I don't know."

"You know what I think?"

"What?"

"Well I hate to say it, but it sounds like your great-grandfather stabbed somebody. With scissors."

"You think?"

"I do. Is that possible? Did you know him?"

"Well I met him, but he died when I was four."

"So you were too young to analyze his true character."

"Like, yeah. I still thought Ronald McDonald was a real person."

"Well, sounds to me like he's stabbed somebody with scissors, and is about to flee the law with his beloved. To avoid the bad destiny of the penitentiary. Wow. Weird weapon, huh? Scissors?"

"Yeah," I said. It felt very bad, to utter that dry, dull 'yeah' instead of my rushing stream of thought. My beautiful bird scissors had been my Great-grampa's weapon! He'd fled with them to the treehouse, and disposed of them in my drawer when he'd met my great-grandmother there to run away with her. This was information that Bridget was entitled to. I felt suddenly lonely, wishing that Bridget and I knew all the same things.

"So who was his victim?" Bridget wondered. "'A life is so easily lost.' It sounds like he killed somebody. Were any of your ancestors murdered?"

"No. Not as far as I know," I said. "Maybe he stabbed somebody and just *thought* they were going to die. He's fleeing, right, so he might not stick around to find out."

"But who was it? Who did he stab?"

"Well, somebody in the Manor," I guessed. "Because he says the house is all bloody."

"That doesn't narrow it down much. 'Cause the Manor was full of people, that book said, when your Great-great-grandfather Magnus had all his big showy parties."

"Maybe my Great-grandfather got drunk and stabbed a guest."

"Or a relative. Could it have been your Great-great-grandfather Magnus? Or your Great-great-aunt Lydia?"

"I guess it could. That would explain why Magnus. . . ." I was about to say it would explain why Magnus cut his son out of the will, but the will was part of what Bridget didn't know. I swallowed my thoughts again.

"It explains. . . ." Bridget prompted.

"It explains the split in the McGrady family," I said. "It explains why Great-great-aunt Lydia wants nothing to do with us."

"Yeah," Bridget agreed. "Because you're the offspring of a violent criminal. No offence."

"You don't think she's scared of us, do you?" I asked.

"Yeah," said Bridget. "I do. Maybe not like real post-traumatic scared. But she probably thinks it's wiser to have nothing to do with you."

I nodded at this new view of Great-great-aunt Lydia. I remembered that one of the words on the torn blue strip was 'afraid'. It was strangely disappointing to think that Great-great-aunt Lydia wasn't some nasty sorceress after all. She was just a nervous old lady.

NOTEBOOK: #25

NAME: Rosamund McGrady

SUBJECT: Visualization

Panther-Lamp Day took over my entire mind. I felt sick to think about Panther-Lamp Day dawning, and the population of Windward Middle School knocking on Great-great-aunt Lydia's door, expecting a tour of Grand Oak Manor.

I thought and thought and thought. In personal skills class, Miss Rankle taught that when you brainstorm for a solution, you write down every idea that occurs to you, no matter how ridiculous. That's why, one desperate afternoon at the treehouse, I wrote "Hold rummage sale at Great-great-aunt Lydia's—pretend it's my house." This idea *was* ridiculous. Great-great-aunt Lydia wanted nothing to do with me or my family. So why would she let me hold a rummage sale at Grand Oak Manor? And how could I convince her to pretend to all the Windward people that I actually lived there? Or if she wouldn't pretend, how could I take every single Panther-Lamp-Day visitor aside, and explain that poor old Great-great-aunt Lydia had lost her mind and couldn't remember anymore who she lived with? I couldn't see how this idea could possibly work. However, as time went on, the severe shortage of better ideas made me keep thinking about it.

Yellow and purple crocuses began sprouting around the trunk of our oak tree. Birds began singing and hopping again in the morning. The bare branches got blurry with buds. These signs of passing time all scared me. The day of the rotating rummage sale was creeping toward me, like the panther on the lamp it was named after.

Another thing Miss Rankle taught in personal skills was visualization. The idea is that by picturing yourself achieving a goal, you help it to come true. I decided to give this advice a try by picturing myself holding a rummage sale at Grand Oak Manor. This turned out to be really hard. I couldn't imagine what Great-great-aunt Lydia and I would be saying to each other; or how she'd be behaving to the visitors; or what stuff we'd be selling or anything. My mental picture was totally lacking in detail, like a bad piece of creative writing. I just couldn't visualize, and according to Miss Rankle, if you don't visualize what you hope for, it's probably not going to happen.

It must have been my determination to visualize that drew me toward Great-great-aunt Lydia's mansion. When the drizzle stopped one cold Monday afternoon in March, I left the treehouse, crossed the meadow and climbed the big cherry tree. From my favourite branch I had a good view over the so-called electric fence. I sat looking through the pale-pink blossoms at the dark grey mansion and the matching dark grey clouds beyond. I sat for a long time, until the damp bark soaked right through my back pockets, but I got no closer to visualization.

I climbed down from the cherry tree and walked through the wet meadow grass toward Grand Oak Manor. I reached the loose board in the so-called electric fence and swung it aside. The turrets loomed above me. I hoped that being so close would make my plan to hold a rummage sale there seem more likely, but it did just the opposite. As I stood outside the fence in the chilly shadow of the Manor, the whole idea seemed impossible. Even so, I couldn't bring myself to turn away and give up on it. I couldn't accept that I had no strategy whatsoever for Panther-Lamp Day. I couldn't go back to the treehouse and just wait for the day to arrive. I couldn't. I'd be surrendering myself to Kendra. I'd be surrendering myself to Devo. And Bridget . . . Bridget and Paige . . . I blocked the thought. I stood at the gap in the fence, putting off the panic that would fill me when I turned away. I don't know how long I'd been there when I heard, over by the stable, the sound of car wheels on Grand Oak Manor's drive. It sounded like the Bentley leaving.

With Great-great-aunt Lydia gone, it was safe to go inside the Manor garden. Maybe entering her space would help me visualize. I was not hopeful, but I was willing to try anything to get back some belief in my stupid Panther-Lamp-Day-at-Grand-Oak-Manor idea. I slipped through the gap in Great-great-aunt Lydia's fence. I squelched down her mossy path, past the fishpond and the deer tree, onto the concrete walkway that outlined the Manor. I skulked along the walkway, my fingers grazing the Manor's rough grey stucco, until I reached a basement window. Kneeling there, I rubbed a patch clean with the sleeve of my fleece jacket. When I stuck my nose up to the cold glass it misted over, and I saw nothing but murk on the other side. I was crouched, waiting for the mist to clear, when I heard heavy breathing. I froze. Behind me, the breathing came closer. My heart beat at hummingbird speed, but I didn't move a muscle. There was a sickening meaty smell and, an instant later, warm, wet breath on the back of my neck. I turned. Inches from my own were the cloudy brown eyeballs of Great-great-aunt Lydia's old basset hound. It was a moment before I realized that Great-great-aunt Lydia was standing there with him.

"Stand up," Great-great-aunt Lydia said. "Stand up, Rosamund, and come with me."

I did as Great-great-aunt Lydia told me. I stood up and I went with her.

I was scared, and I thought about running. Great-great-aunt Lydia was extremely slow, so I could obviously outrun her. But maybe, I thought, I was *meant* to be found by her there, outside the Manor. Maybe this was visualization turning things into reality! Great-great-aunt Lydia led me along the concrete walkway, her sensible shoes crushing the little yellow weeds in the cracks. At old-lady pace we went up the big front steps, and across the threshold. As I stepped into the unknown space of Grand Oak Manor and heard the door close behind me I had a sudden sense of captivity, as though I'd been swallowed by a whale. I fought an urge to leave. I would get no other chance, before Panther-Lamp Day, to befriend Great-great-aunt Lydia.

She brought me down a long, long hallway to a gigantic room, deep within the Manor. At the doorway she paused and changed direction. "This way," she said, and led me up a castle-type staircase. She opened the door to a small room that had six walls, like the treehouse. I realized it was the turret. "This will do," Great-great-aunt Lydia said. "Sit down."

I sat in an armchair that rose about a yard above my head. It had a cushion like a sack of concrete. I folded my hands in my lap. Obedience was my strategy. I hoped that my perfect behaviour would demonstrate to Great-great-aunt Lydia that I was nothing like my maniac murderer of a great-grampa. The basset hound lay down beside me, rested his head on his front paws, and shut his eyes. "Wait here," Great-great-aunt Lydia said, and she left the room, clicking the door shut behind her.

I waited with the patience of the obedient. On the table beside me were a pair of binoculars, and a pen, and a box of blue stationery.

*From the Desk of*
*Lydia Florence Augustine McGrady*
*Grand Oak Manor*
*Number 9 Bellemonde Drive*

On the other side of the turret was the desk that the stationery was talking about. I wanted to tiptoe over to look, but I didn't want to risk my obedient image. I could see the treehouse through the spring foliage of our far-off oak tree, and I wished I was there.

Great-great-aunt Lydia was gone a long time. I started

to wonder what was going on. Then I thought of something. *Trespassers Will Be Prosecuted*. I'd never taken that sign any more seriously than the one that said *Warning—Electric Fence*, but I began to take it seriously then. Was it possible, I wondered, that when Great-great-aunt Lydia had told me to come with her, she was conducting a citizen's arrest? Had she gone to call the police? She *had*, I thought, and she was waiting for them to arrive. They would take me to the police station, and after that I would be prosecuted in Youth Court, where I had been warning Tilley that she and Eveline would end up. At Youth Court, there would be a crime reporter from the local newspaper, and then when we studied current events in social studies my whole class would read about how I had a criminal record for trespassing at the house I claimed to live in. It would be even more humiliating than Panther-Lamp Day.

Should I leave, I wondered. If I left and managed to find my way out of the mansion, Great-great-aunt Lydia would not be able to prove my trespass beyond a reasonable doubt. But *could* I leave? I remembered that click of the turret door. Had it been the click of a lock? Was I imprisoned there, among the worn out fancy furniture, in the dim afternoon? Had Great-great-aunt Lydia's basset hound been left behind to guard me?

At my feet the basset hound breathed slowly. "Hey boy," I said, stroking his neck in a careful test of ferocity. "Hey there! Hello boy! Good dog!" I said, scritching under his collar. Without lifting his head, the basset hound opened one eye, then shut it again. I felt better for a moment, until new thoughts formed.

I had come inside with Great-great-aunt Lydia to show that, unlike my violent great-grandfather, I was nice and she didn't have to be nervous. But if Great-great-aunt Lydia was nervous, would she have brought me inside the Manor all by herself? I had written Great-grampa Tavish's letter out in normal format, and I took it from my wallet.

I did not ever think a pair of scissors could do
so much harm. I have to leave this bloody house.
A bad destiny awaits me here.
A life is so easily lost.
Let us escape. Let us elope.
Isobel meet me: the treehouse at ten.

X.

I had interpreted the letter the way Bridget did, because Bridget was smart. But I had not given Bridget all the facts. Come to think of it, some of the facts that I had given her were wrong. There was another way to read the letter, I realized. Maybe Great-great-aunt Lydia was the one wielding the scissors. Maybe *she* had done the harm. Maybe Great-grampa had escaped to save himself. Maybe his own murder was the bad destiny awaiting him at Grand Oak Manor. My scalp prickled. Maybe, I thought, I should get out of here.

NOTEBOOK: #26

NAME: Rosamund McGrady

SUBJECT: Afternoon Tea

Just as I'd decided to flee the doorknob turned. In the turret doorway stood Great-great-aunt Lydia, in her tartan skirt and her knit stockings that were like athletic bandages. She looked so old and incapable of harm that my fears suddenly seemed crazy. Fleeing seemed rude. I stayed in my chair.

Great-great-aunt Lydia crossed the room. She took small, careful steps, as if checking the floor for booby traps. Finally she reached the armchair opposite mine. She sat down in ultra slow motion, all except for the last couple of inches, which were speeded up by the force of gravity. She gave me a long look. Her face had no expression at all, only wrinkles.

A man entered the turret. He was not a police officer. He was old, and he was wearing a cardigan and a tie. It was the same man who had been with the workman putting up signs on the so-called electric fence. I recognized his hair, gushing out of his head in big grey waves. He advanced on us with two mugs and a stout brown teapot.

"Not *that* one, Mr. Bickert," Great-great-aunt Lydia said. This time she did have an expression, which was annoyance. "The good teapot! The *good* one! And tea*cups*, not mugs!"

Mr. Bickert pursed his mouth, nodded once, and disappeared with his tray.

Great-great-aunt Lydia looked at me. "I've been waiting for you Rosamund."

"Waiting for me?"

"Waiting for you to come back."

"Come back?" I repeated.

"You left so suddenly, that time you were here," Great-great-aunt Lydia said. "Just an introduction, and then you were gone. I expect I scared you away somehow. I've thought and thought, but I never could determine how. I expect I was curt, was I? I know I can be curt. Heaven knows, I've been told."

She meant the time that Paige had driven me home and I had hugged her at the front door of Grand Oak Manor. "No," I said. "No, you weren't curt. I just—dropped by to say hello. That's all."

"Ah," said Great-great-aunt Lydia. "I'd hoped you were accepting my invitation."

"Invitation?" I asked.

"Yes. My invitation to afternoon tea."

"I never got an invitation to afternoon tea," I said. "I would have come if I had."

"You most certainly did get an invitation to afternoon tea," she said. "With the flowers, on the day you moved in."

"We got the flowers," I said. "And thank you, they were so pretty. But there was no invitation with them." Before I could mention the torn letter in the stream, Great-great-aunt Lydia spoke again, the turkey wattles of her neck swinging with her words.

"Nonsense! There was. I attached it to the arrangement myself. My memory may not be what it was, but that I am sure of." She pushed herself out of her hard throne. At her desk she picked up a file. She turned toward me, a shaking paper in her hand. "Just as I said. The invitation. I keep a copy of all my correspondence, Rosamund, and I'd advise you to do the same. It's useful when disputes arise, as they so often do."

She handed me the paper. It was a photocopy of a letter on her stationery.

*From the Desk of*
*Lydia Florence Augustine McGrady*
*Grand Oak Manor*
*Number 9 Bellemonde Drive*

June 30

To the McGrady family:

I must confess it was a shock to hear from family lost so long.

I had forgotten the clause about the treehouse, if I ever knew of it.

I am afraid that I felt some suspicion, and called my lawyers.

I do hope you won't be offended. They took the will from archives. It turns out to be authentic, the copy that you unknowingly possessed all these years. They considered whether in law the treehouse is indeed yours, as you four now claim that it is. It turns out that it is. They checked also to see whether in fact you are who you say you are. Of course, as you know full well, it turns out that you are. So, finally, I am in a position to reply. Please forgive my tardiness. To the treehouse, meadow and woods, you are welcome. I've not been there in many long years in any case, since old bones like mine are broken easily in a fall on rough ground. I nonetheless hope we'll become acquainted. Please accept my invitation for lunch or afternoon tea here at Grand Oak Manor someday soon. Please write or ring me at (406) 189 4666.

Yours truly,

Lydia McGrady

I recognized some of the words from the torn blue strip we had found in the stream. Great-great-aunt Lydia lowered herself carefully back into her chair, free-falling the last couple of inches. "There. That's one invitation we've confirmed that you received. As well as the verbal one my manservant delivered the time I saw you and your sister by the hedge. Perhaps you'll be so good as to tell me why you chose not to come."

I was too scared of Great-great-aunt Lydia to insist that we'd never received her letter, and that Mr. Bickert had never spoken to Tilley and me. "I just—got the feeling that you didn't want to know us," I said.

"Why ever did you think that?"

"Um. Well. I guess maybe because you didn't answer our party invitation."

"Your party invitation! What party invitation? I got no party invitation. I don't receive so many that I could have forgotten, I'm quite sure of that."

"Well, we mailed it. Mom said she mailed it. And then there were the signs."

"The *signs*?"

"The signs telling us to stay away."

"What *are* you saying? That some silly omen told you to avoid Grand Oak Manor?"

"No," I said. "I mean actual, physical signs. The signs on your fence."

"Signs on my fence? There are no signs on my fence," Great-great-aunt Lydia said. "*Signs on my fence.* Grand Oak Manor isn't a shopping mall."

I still didn't have the nerve to argue. "Oh," I said. "Maybe I imagined it. Somehow I just thought I saw some signs."

"Saying *what*?" she asked.

"Um. Well. I think they were about trespassing," I said. "That is, I *thought* they were. But you must be right. I mean, you know what's on your own fence, obviously."

"*Is* that obvious?" Great-great-aunt Lydia considered. "It's really not, you know. I *don't* know what's on my fence, now that I think of it. Not on the outside. Not first hand. I haven't been out into the meadow for years. Not since my hip replacement."

"But. . . ."

"But what, Rosamund?"

"But then, how did you leave us the flowers?"

"Through my manservant, of course. It's Mr. Bickert who makes the deliveries to the treehouse. Not that there have been many. Just the Christmas card, and the posie of herbs when you were so ill."

She meant the dead plants stabbed to the tree. "What were they for?" I asked. "The herbs?"

"What were they for! They were for exactly what I

described in some detail in the letter attached to them. They were medicinal herbs, for boiling. There is nothing like them to clear the lungs and sinuses. Don't tell me you didn't try them."

I didn't tell her that I didn't try them. I also didn't tell her that there had been no letter attached. I didn't want *that* argument all over again. "Yes, no, you're so right," I said. "I've never tasted anything like them."

"*Tasted*! They're not for drinking, those herbs, they're for medicinal *steam*. Really, Rosamund, you should pay more attention to the written word. It's a wonder you didn't poison yourself, and make yourself even sicker than you were."

"How did you know I was sick?" I asked.

Great-great-aunt Lydia nodded at the binoculars that sat on the table beside us. "I have a good vantage point from here," she said. "And plenty of opportunity to observe. To put it mildly. You didn't leave the treehouse for days. I was concerned. It was quite the relief to see you again, crossing the meadow to your outhouse."

Mr. Bickert appeared in the doorway of the turret. Instead of his tray he had a trolley with a silver teapot about the size of a fire hydrant. There were also flowered teacups, and a sugar bowl and cream jug, trimmed in gold.

"Mr. Bickert," Great-great-aunt Lydia said sharply. "Tell me what you know about *No Trespassing* signs on my fence."

"*No Trespassing* signs?" he asked. He looked from Great-great-aunt Lydia to me, and back to her again. "*No Trespassing* signs. Hmmm. I don't believe I know anything about *No Trespassing* signs."

I distinctly remembered seeing him hand one to the workman, so I knew that he was lying. Besides, you could tell by the way his eyes were zipping all around. They reminded me of minnows that have just been caught in a saucepan. Maybe Mr. Bickert was feeling a bit like those minnows. Great-great-aunt Lydia was watching him carefully.

"What exactly did they say, Rosamund?" Great-great-aunt Lydia asked, without looking away from Mr. Bickert.

"*Trespassers Will Be Prosecuted*," I said. It seemed embarrassing to quote the ones about the guard dog and the electric fence.

"'*Trespassers Will Be Prosecuted*'," she repeated. "Tell me about *those* signs, Mr. Bickert."

Mr. Bickert frowned and closed his eyes and drummed his fingers against his temples. "Oh, the *signs*," he said. "Oh, wait a moment, now, I *do* remember something about signs! That's right! The fence-builders put them up. Of course, I just assumed they said *Fence by Wedgewood Construction* or something of that nature. *Trespassers Will Be Prosecuted*! Dear, dear, dear. I had no idea."

"No idea, Mr. Bickert?" Great-great-aunt Lydia asked. "No idea such as scaring off my next of kin? No idea, such as keeping potential heirs away until I'm safely dead?"

"Certainly *not,* Madam," he said, doing a shocked face. "Why, I'm *delighted* to have your young great-great-niece as our visitor." He switched from his shocked face to give me a bare-toothed smile. It was so phony it looked like someone had cut it out of a magazine and stuck it on his face.

"No doubt," Great-great-aunt Lydia said.

Mr. Bickert clutched the humongous teapot as though it were his only friend. "Milk and sugar, Rosamund?" he asked.

"Yes, please. Four sugars," I said. He poured the tea and handed me a fancy cup. He handed another to Great-great-aunt Lydia, and left us alone.

She raised her teacup almost to her lips, but she didn't sip. She stared into the teacup as though she had forgotten what to do with it. "The fence," she said very quietly. "I wonder if Mr. Bickert told me the right thing, about this legal advice that I was to build a fence. I just wonder now."

She took a sip from her teacup, put it down, and looked at me. "Well. Grand Oak Manor can't have seemed very welcoming," she said. I could see that she was trying to smile, but she seemed sort of out of practice.

I shrugged. "I thought it was because of our family's big split."

"Our big split," Great-great-aunt Lydia said. "Is that what your parents call it? And what do they say about it, the big split?"

"Not much, really. Dad doesn't even know what caused it, so he mostly just wonders." I hesitated. "I wonder too."

"You wonder, do you?" Great-great-aunt Lydia was silent for a while. "Well, it has affected your family a great deal, there's no doubt of that. And I suppose you'll never know if I don't tell you. So I will tell you, Rosamund, if that's what you want." I nodded. She lifted her rattling cup for a sip. I felt a thrill, because I knew the story I was about to hear would be a genuine grown-up drama.

"Well," she began. "Your great-grandfather was a young man when the falling out occurred. He was still living at Grand Oak Manor then, along with me and Father. Your great-grandfather, Tavish, was my younger brother—I expect you know that. A year and a half younger, although he always seemed much younger than that. In those days I enjoyed my needlework and I had bought myself some special scissors. They were very well-made scissors, razor sharp." She paused and stared at the shreds of steam rising from her cup. I waited in suspense for the violent part. Great-great-aunt Lydia took a sip and spoke again.

"My scissors suddenly disappeared. When I asked Tavish about them he said he had no recollection of any scissors, but that didn't convince me he hadn't taken them. He was a scatterbrain, Tavish. Eventually, it occurred to me to search the treehouse, the one you live in today. Of course, Tavish ought to have outgrown the treehouse by that age, but even at seventeen he often slept there. He always was mad for that treehouse. You see, he was not a very serious young man: certainly not so serious as Father would have liked. Father had great plans for Tavish. He intended Tavish to take over the family lumber business. He intended Tavish to take his place in high society. Tavish would have none of it. He didn't want to 'lose his life' to Father's plans, was how he insisted upon putting it. Always dramatic, was Tavish. Where was I?"

"The scissors," I reminded her.

"Oh yes, the scissors. Well, as I say, I searched the treehouse, and there I found them, in the drawer of his bunk. He'd borrowed them, the way he borrowed everything else. There was hardly a thing I owned that he didn't borrow. No sense of property at all. And not only had he borrowed my scissors, he'd damaged them. The blades were all askew. I can only think that he used them to cut rope. They were useless for needlework in that condition, which distressed me. I should add that these were very beautiful scissors—"

"With gold handles shaped like a bird, and blades for a beak," I supplied.

"How did you know?" Great-great-aunt Lydia asked.

"I found them when we moved in," I said.

"That's right," she said. "That's right. I left them there, to prove my point that they'd become useless to me. I recall doing that now. So now you know how they got there. And now you know the story of the split, as you call it, in the McGrady family."

She stopped and sipped her tea. I did not see how that could possibly be the end of the story. "But I don't get . . . ," I said. "I mean, a pair of scissors . . . I don't see how. . . ."

"Oh. Yes. Well, I was furious with Tavish, of course. I got Father on my side. That was always easy for me to do. And it always *was* important to me, to have Father on my side. Father and I both let Tavish know what we thought about him ruining the scissors. Of course, we went beyond the scissors. The scissors just showed his character, we told him. His irresponsible character. It was nothing we hadn't said to him many times before. And he came with us to the opera that afternoon, just as usual. But in his mind there must have been something different about that particular scolding, because the next morning we discovered that he'd run away in the night. Father was furious, of course. But it was such an impulsive thing that we expected Tavish to come back. To '*come crawling back*', is what Father expected. But he never did. And I never spoke to him again. Nor did Father."

"Wow," I said, totally shocked. I had fully expected to be

shocked when I finally heard the cause of the family split. But I'd expected to be shocked at the great big adult seriousness of it, and what shocked me was just the opposite.

"You're surprised, Rosamund?" Great-great-aunt Lydia asked.

"Well, yes," I admitted. "I mean, borrowing scissors. I just—I don't know—like—I mean—I just wouldn't expect something like that to cause a fight that lasts a whole lifetime."

"No. No. One doesn't expect it," she said. "The thing about a life, though, is that it passes one moment at a time. And no single one of those moments seems the perfect one to end a quarrel."

I nodded, thinking about my fight with Tilley, and we both got all quiet.

"When Great-grampa ran away," I asked. "Was he by himself?"

"Was he by himself. Well. No. He was not."

"Was he with girl called Isobel?"

"He was with your great-grandmother, yes."

"What was she like?"

"I can't say. I didn't know her. She wasn't of our class at all. She was an usherette at the Orpheum Theater. I'd seen her there, but I knew her name only by her name tag. Father could never fathom how Tavish had gotten to know her, with him being such a watchful parent. I never quite mustered the courage to tell Father about the note I'd found, oh, half a year before the elopement. I'd found it folded up inside Tavish's glove the afternoon we'd seen Madame Butterfly. It said something about meeting at night at the treehouse. I questioned Tavish, naturally, and he managed to convince me that the note was from a school chum. It wasn't signed, you see. And I was naïve, nothing like young women are today. I never guessed that a young man from the top rung of society would throw his future away on a girl with no advantages. It was only looking back, after he was gone, that I realized. Tavish and Isobel had probably been meeting in the treehouse for some time."

I nodded. Her finding the note in the glove explained why Great-grampa had started using a code. I thought of mentioning the coded letter, but decided not to. Great-grampa had said it was a bad destiny, to lose his life by living it with her and Magnus at Grand Oak Manor. That could only hurt her feelings.

"I've given you nothing to eat," Great-great-aunt Lydia said. "Children like to eat, after school, as I recall. I'll have Mr. Bickert bring something." I expected her to ring some kind of old-fashioned bell, but instead she unclipped a cell phone from the waistband of her tartan skirt.

"Mr. Bickert. Something to eat with our tea please." She replaced the cell phone and turned to me. "Now tell me, Rosamund. Knowing of the family split, as you call it, and seeing the *No Trespassing* signs, what were you *doing* at Grand Oak Manor? Why were you at my basement window?"

I told her. I thought she had been surprisingly honest, so I took a deep breath and told the truth, too. I told her how I'd accidentally made Bridget believe I lived in Grand Oak Manor, and how it was too late to change my story, and how everybody wanted to visit Grand Oak Manor on Panther-Lamp Day.

The door opened and Mr. Bickert came in carrying a

three-storey serving platter. I expected fancy goodies on a platter like this, but when he came closer I saw that each story was filled with those plain beige biscuits that babies and old people eat. The bottom storey had round ones, the middle storey had square ones, and the top storey had oval. Mr. Bickert fussed around, putting down little serving plates, and offering the biscuits, and pouring more tea, and adding milk, and clutching sugar lumps with tiny clawed tongs. I didn't want to talk with him there, but I was afraid that if I waited for him to leave the subject would have changed from Panther-Lamp Day, and my chance would be gone.

"So I was wondering, Great-great-aunt Lydia," I said. "I know you barely know me, and I know it's a lot to ask, but I was wondering if I could maybe possibly hold Panther-Lamp Day here at Grand Oak Manor."

"Hold it here?" Great-great-aunt Lydia asked. "If that would solve your problem, then yes, Rosamund, you may."

The next part I *really* didn't want to say with Mr. Bickert standing there, but he was rearranging the biscuits on the three-storey platter, and he showed no signs of leaving. I think he wanted to listen.

"And would it be okay," I asked, "if I pretended to live here?"

Great-great-aunt Lydia paused. "I'd be pleased for you to tell people that this is your home," she answered finally. "I'd be pleased for you to *consider* it your home." At this Mr. Bickert froze at his cookie-arranging like a DVD on pause.

"Thank you," I said. "Thank you very much. Like, very, *very* much. And I'm sorry to keep asking for favours, but there's one more. Which is that we really don't have any extra stuff for the sale, and I was wondering if you had any old things that you'd like me to sell for you."

"You need things to sell? Just grab an armload of whatever you see." Great-great-aunt Lydia waved her veiny hand at the china vases and the oil paintings and the gilt-framed mirrors. "I've seen it all for ninety-one years and I don't need to see it any more."

Mr. Bickert was moving again, but he didn't look happy. He was rearranging his rearrangement of biscuits.

"The biscuits are a work of art, Mr. Bickert," Great-great-aunt Lydia said. "You may be excused." Nodding and pursing his lips, Mr. Bickert left. "Now, Rosamund," she said when he was gone. "You must tell me all about how you manage in the treehouse. I've been able to determine some things through my binoculars, but of course so much can't be seen. I want to hear everything." When I started describing our life in the treehouse, Great-great-aunt Lydia seemed really interested. She said that we were resourceful, and she said that we were clever, and she nodded and nodded. After awhile her eyelids drooped, and then on one of her nods her head just didn't come up again.

"Great-great-aunt Lydia," I said. Deathly silence. "Great-great-aunt Lydia," I said again, and this time she gave a single snore. I called her name a few more times, and I even jiggled her arm. I tried for five minutes, but I couldn't wake her up. She was still slumped and snoring in her wing-backed chair when I left the turret. I tiptoed down the great hallway. I hoped to avoid Mr. Bickert, but when I stepped outside the front door, there he was. He had a pipe in his mouth, and he stared down at me. His nostrils curled with smoke, like a person from a nether world. There was a musky, sweet, smoldering smell. It was the Halloween smell from the Manor garden.

"She's asleep," I told Mr. Bickert.

"Asleep, is she? All the *stress*, I expect. Well, you'd best be off, *Rosamund*," he said, and the way he said "Rosamund" you'd think it was a swearword. "I think you've caused quite enough *excitement* for one day."

He left his pipe on a stone urn and stepped inside the front door. It seemed to close very quickly behind me. Outside it had gotten darker and colder. I squelched along the mossy path and slipped between the loose boards of the fence. Looking over my shoulder at Mr. Bickert's *No Trespassing* signs, I headed into the twilight. As I reached the orchard I felt a weird sensation. I had a sense of myself as tiny in the vast meadow, as if observed from a distance. Shivering like the new cherry blossoms, I hurried across the meadow to the treehouse.

NOTEBOOK: #27

NAME: Rosamund McGrady

SUBJECT: Enemy Watches

As I climbed the ladder to the treehouse, my head swirled with discovery. There was no violent drama in the McGrady family. That was not what had caused the big split. The big split was about a pair of borrowed scissors. The big split was about, when you got right down to it, nothing at all. And Great-great-aunt Lydia had wanted to get to know us all along. She hadn't tried to keep us away. Mr. Bickert had just tried to make it look that way, because he hoped that if he could keep Great-great-aunt Lydia completely alone, he would inherit all her money. It was Mr. Bickert who had ripped up Great-great-aunt Lydia's welcome letter and thrown it in the stream. It was Mr. Bickert who'd arranged the fence and the *No Trespassing* signs. It was Mr. Bickert who had taken Great-great-aunt Lydia's get well card, and him who had stabbed her medicinal herb posie to our oak tree. It was Mr. Bickert who had lurked quietly in the dark garden on

Halloween. It was Mr. Bickert who had taken Great-great-aunt Lydia's Christmas card and left just the empty envelope. The evil that we'd sensed around Grand Oak Manor had all been Mr. Bickert's. These were my thoughts as I butted open the rain-swollen treehouse door.

Mom, Dad and Tilley sat at the folding table, shelling peas. "Rosie, what is it," Mom said as I stood in the arched doorway.

"What's what?"

"You look all dazzled. You look like you're bursting with news."

I *was* bursting with news, and the three of them would be fascinated to hear it.

"No. No news," I said. I was dying to talk about what had just happened, but it was better not to. If I told, my parents would find out I'd trespassed in the Manor garden, but that wasn't really what kept me quiet. What really kept me quiet was Tilley. It would be a mistake to share my knowledge with her. Knowledge is power, and Tilley had too much power already. If I told her about Great-great-aunt Lydia, she'd probably specify that I had to bring her and Eveline to Grand Oak Manor, and then visiting Grand Oak Manor would feel just like all the lunchtime trips to Lester's Pizza Hideaway. Knowledge was power, and power was something I was missing. I didn't want to tell Tilley anything anymore, which meant that I couldn't tell my parents much either. None of them even knew that Great-great-aunt Lydia's coded letter had been solved. I turned from my family and peeled potatoes at the counter that circled the oak branch.

Three days later I went back to Grand Oak Manor to

work out the details of Panther-Lamp Day. I didn't let the glaring brass lady on the door knocker intimidate me: I rapped on the thick front door. Mr. Bickert answered, with an expression exactly like the door knocker. "May I please see Great-great-aunt Lydia?" I asked. He didn't answer right away. I'll bet he was thinking of how to get rid of me. He must have been scared that he wouldn't get away with it though, because eventually he invited me in and went off to get her. I stood in the big entranceway and listened to the grandfather clock measuring out time. Great-great-aunt Lydia appeared at the end of the hall, about half a block away. Slowly she made her way toward me.

"You're back, Rosamund," she said when she finally got within talking distance. "I've been thinking about your Panther-Lamp Day. I've put together a few things for you to sell. Come have a look." She opened the huge hall wardrobe to show me shelves of dishes and lace and candle-holders and stuff. "Will these be suitable?" she asked. They looked like the kind of things the Windward mothers would go nuts over.

"Totally suitable," I said. "Those will be *great*. Thank you very much for doing all this."

"Oh, you're perfectly welcome," Great-great-aunt Lydia said. "It gives me something new to think about, this Panther-Lamp Day of yours."

"There's something else about Panther-Lamp Day that I forgot to tell you last time," I said. I explained how I'd pretended to the Hanrahans that we were renovating a family room.

"You do complicate things, don't you, Rosamund," she said. "Well, come along then. I'll show you what rooms

I've got, and you can pick one to be your family room." Walking at old lady speed, we went around to all the rooms on the main floor. Every single one of these rooms was so much like every other that I wondered why anybody would want so many of them. They were all very stiff and fancy. None of them was much like a family room, so I just chose the biggest. "So this is to be your family room, is it? This used to be our ballroom," Great-great-aunt Lydia said. "I danced in this room with the Prince of Wales. I'll bet you can't imagine me dancing, can you?" She smiled. Either I was getting used to her, or she was getting a bit better at smiling. The ballroom did not look as if it had been recently renovated. As fancy as it was, it actually looked a bit dingy. This didn't worry me. I planned to say that the decorators had worked hard to achieve an authentic antique look.

"There's just one more thing," I said as we stood in the ballroom doorway. My heart thumped with apology. "When I told Bridget that my family lived at Grand Oak Manor? I also told her that you *don't* live here. I said that you ran away from Grand Oak Manor years ago. I'm sorry." Great-great-aunt Lydia's face didn't change but it did: it was like watching a landscape shadow with arriving cloud.

"Did you now?" said Great-great-aunt Lydia. "Then I suppose you're asking me to keep out of sight on Panther-Lamp Day?"

That would definitely be the simplest for me, but it was too hard and mean to ask Great-great-aunt Lydia to hide inside her own house, especially when she was doing so much to help me. "No," I said. "No. I'll just tell Bridget that we met and made up and got over the past. I'll tell her that we're all here together now. That we're one big family."

"Yes," said Great-great-aunt Lydia. "Yes, I like that better."

Great-great-aunt Lydia and I worked out the final details of Panther-Lamp Day in the turret, over tea and beige biscuits. The merchandise would be on the Manor's long, long dining room table. Great-great-aunt Lydia and I would handle sales together. Panther-Lamp Day visitors would be permitted to tour the main floor of the Manor, but not the upper floor. An exception would be made for Bridget and Paige. Great-great-aunt Lydia would show them the upstairs, including two rooms that she'd pretend were Tilley's and mine. Beforehand I'd bring clothes and other props for these two bedrooms. For added authenticity I'd recreate bedroom mess.

"And you may rest assured, Rosamund, that before I meet the Hanrahans I'll invent the life that I led after you have me running away. I'm quite looking forward to it, really. The possibilities are endless."

When Great-great-aunt Lydia and I finished our tea she saw me to the Manor's big front door. Mr. Bickert held my fleece jacket for me to put on, and I flailed my arms for the sleeves. "I do hope you'll come again before this Panther-Lamp Day," Great-great-aunt Lydia said, and Mr. Bickert wrinkled his mouth. I had started down the front steps when Great-great-aunt Lydia spoke again. "Don't I get one of your fierce hugs?" she asked. She meant the one I'd given her the time that Paige had driven me. I ran up three steps and hugged her, and she gave me a crepe-papery kiss on the cheek. Mr. Bickert turned away.

On the way through the Manor garden I passed the fishpond. The fish swam to the surface as if they hoped to eat me alive. "No humans for you today," I told them. I slipped through the gap in Mr. Bickert's fence and headed back to the treehouse. Spring was all around me. There were stunt-flying birds; there were daffodils sprouting so close together on the meadow that I could hardly take a step without squashing one; there were big, pink clouds of cherry blossoms against the blue sky. These signs of spring no longer filled me with dread, now that the problem of Panther-Lamp Day was solved.

Spring is fickle. The next morning it was raining hard enough for the hideous rain gear. Except for the plastic rustle of our capes, Tilley and I rode toward school in silence. She and I didn't talk much anymore. As we crossed the plank bridge over the stream I saw six fluffy new ducklings with beaks the size of sunflower seeds, pecking at the landing raindrops as though they were food. They were so cute it was almost heartbreaking, but I didn't even point them out to Tilley. I didn't say anything either about the blue carpet of periwinkle, or about the new pink salmonberry blossoms lighting up the dark green woods. Neither did Tilley. She knew better than to try to make happy springtime talk with me.

Near the end of the path I locked my bike. I was getting my umbrella out of the hollow tree when Tilley spoke. It was the first time either of us had said anything since leaving home. "Do you feel like there's someone watching us?"

"How can you *feel* someone watching you?" I scoffed.

"You know,"Tilley said. "Like little prickly dots on the back of your neck, sort of."

"That's stupid," I said. At the very end of the path I looked through salmonberry leaves.

"See?" I said, stepping out of the woods. "Nobody." I put up my umbrella and led Tilley down the sidewalk to Sir Combover Elementary.

After school I went to Bridget's. "What do you feel like doing?" Bridget asked. "Do you want to map out where to go on Panther-Lamp Day?"

"Actually," I said. "Actually, I won't be able to tour the other sales. I have to do sales at Grand Oak Manor. The most amazing thing has happened."

"What?"

"Great-great-aunt Lydia. She's not mad at my family, and she's living at Grand Oak Manor. And she wants me to man the sales table with her on Panther-Lamp Day." These were all true statements, if only I could have left them at that.

"*What?* Rosie, you're leaving a million things out! How did this happen?"

I felt such a longing to tell the truth. The truth was expanding within me, and I knew that the only way to relieve the pressure would be to tell it. Plus the truth seemed so nice and simple, with all the details ready-made and included. But so much of the truth did not fit with what I'd told Bridget so far. I took a deep breath. Oxygenated, I began my story.

I said that Mom had run into Great-great-aunt Lydia at the supermarket, and recognized her from old family pictures. I knew stories needed convincing details, so I said that Mom and Great-great-aunt Lydia were waiting for the chickens to finish roasting. I said that there had been regular chickens already roasted, but that they'd looked dry and stringy, so Mom had decided to wait for the free run chickens to finish their circuit on the rotisserie, even though they were three dollars more.

"Who cares about roast chickens," Bridget said. "What did they *say* to each other? That's what I want to know."

But here I got vague. They'd said it was a shame that they'd lost touch, I told Bridget, and Great-great-aunt Lydia said that she didn't like her old age home, and Mom said to come and live at Grand Oak Manor, where the whole McGrady family belonged.

"Just like that? Bizarre!"

"It takes awhile to roast a chicken," I pointed out. "It was a long conversation."

"And she's already moved in with you guys? When?"

I picked the day that I'd met Great-great-aunt Lydia. "Monday," I said.

Bridget stared. "She's been living with you all *week* and you didn't tell me? I can't believe it."

I stared back, consciously trying to make my face look honest.

"What does she say about your great-grampa?" Bridget wanted to know. "Who did he attack with the scissors?"

"She doesn't want to talk about him," I said. To this, Bridget said not a single thing. I changed the subject and chatted the way I wished Bridget would, but she was quiet the rest of the afternoon. Paige invited me to stay for Chinese food and I did. I watched Bridget's straight-ahead profile as she knit at her chow mein with her chopsticks.

Bridget's fortune cookie said "A friend will surprise you." Mine said "An enemy watches."

I left soon after dinner, but I didn't go straight home. Somehow having a head full of private knowledge made me want to be alone. The library was the only place I could think to go. I saw Kendra there checking out a stack of teen Cosmos, but we ignored each other. I sat reading in the cookbook aisle. At library closing the air was dark with rain and I hurried along the sidewalk to the start of the path. Entering the woods, I found myself in gloom. I fished out my headlamp and switched it on. Dropping my umbrella into the hollow tree, I pulled out my hideous cape and shook out possible bugs. As I bent to unchain my bike from the pine tree, I saw in the weak beam of my headlamp that my rear tire was flat. I left my bike there and began to walk. I'd have to hurry to make it home on foot before dark.

I hadn't gone twenty yards down the path when I felt it. It was exactly what Tilley had described: prickly dots on the back of my neck. I turned and looked behind me. There was nothing but the thickening gloom. I was being stupid, I told myself. I kept on walking.

Raindrops pattered on my hood, and my cape crackled with each step. And then I heard it: the snap of a branch behind me. I stopped and turned right around, but I couldn't see anything but darkening woods. They looked fairy-tale creepy. The snap had been a branch falling, I told myself. Branches *do* fall all by themselves—that was how I got my Christmas boughs. I pushed my hood from my head and rustled off again, faster than before. I had my ears on full alert by this time, but I heard only the overpowering crackle of my hideous cape. And then: *snap*. Again. Closer behind me than last time.

"Hello," I called out. My voice wobbled into the woods. There was no answer but raindrops. Maybe it was a coyote, I thought. I flapped my hideous cape, hoping to scare the coyote with its plastic crackle and its pure orange weirdness. I rustled off again. I felt like running, but I didn't, because that would make the coyote think I was prey. I forced myself to walk at normal speed, but I kept looking over my shoulder.

Then I heard other sounds. Another snap. A soft thud, like a stumble. A jangle, like keys.

"Who's there?" I meant to sound challenging, but I sounded like someone who couldn't put up a good fight. Could the jangle be dog tags? I wanted to run, but running from dogs is not good either. I had to find out what was behind me. A few steps later I twirled around. I had only an impression of pale movement by the enormous stump: it was so fleeting that I couldn't tell whether it happened in my peripheral vision or just in my imagination.

"Who's there?" I called. There was silence and there were woods. I reached into my pocket for the folding knife that had skewered Great-great-aunt Lydia's posie of medicinal herbs. Without looking down I opened the blade. I listened and I watched. The longer I listened and the longer I watched, the more imaginary it seemed, that flesh-pale glimpse. Softly I moved to the left, distantly circling the stump. I would make sure there was nothing there and then I would continue home, reassured. Each leftward step brought a new view of dark stump, each one hardly different from the last. Then I stepped again and saw it, resting on an old logger's cut. It was there, and then it withdrew and was gone. It was brief, but there was no mistaking it. It was a hand. It was human.

| | |
|---|---|
| NOTEBOOK: | #28 |
| NAME: | Rosamund McGrady |
| SUBJECT: | Caught |

Run, my mind shrieked, and I did. I flung off my cape and ran until the woods blurred. I ran up the ramp over the stone wall, across the plank bridge and through the meadow. I never slowed down to look behind me, and it was impossible to say whether the thump-thump-thumping I heard was pursuing footsteps or my own pumping heart. I reached the oak tree and climbed the ladder like I was on fast-forward.

"Rosie, what is it?" Mom said as I burst through the treehouse door. "What's wrong?"

"Somebody's. After me," I gasped. "Somebody. Chased me. In the woods."

Dad grabbed the big flashlight and clambered down to the meadow. We all ran through the woods to where my hideous cape lay in the wet dirt like evidence at a crime scene. Dad moved through the trees swinging the flashlight. Shadows swooped away from the light, but nothing else moved. Whoever was stalking me had gone.

That night I lay in my middle bunk listening to Tilley creak above me. I thought about my stalker. It was possible that he was a classic weirdo: the kind who came out as soon as it was dark, just as Paige had warned. I did not believe that, however. I believed that my stalker was Mr. Bickert. Mr. Bickert had a motive: he wanted to prevent me from getting to know Great-great-aunt Lydia. But plain old stalking wouldn't be enough for him. To be certain of keeping me away from Great-great-aunt Lydia, Mr. Bickert really needed me dead. In the pure, long-lasting darkness of the night, I started believing that I'd narrowly avoided my own murder. I opened the little pocket knife that Mr. Bickert had stuck in the oak tree, and I placed it at my bunkside. I listened hard to the silence, convinced that every nighttime sound was Mr. Bickert coming to finish me off. Stiff with fear, I'd get my headlamp ready. I imagined Mr. Bickert caught in its beam, with his cardigan and his tie and his murder weapon. This mental image was so vivid that when I pressed the "on" button I was almost startled to see that he was not there. That's how I spent the entire night. It wasn't until the sky paled with dawn that I considered it safe to fall asleep.

I slept in the next morning. When I woke up the sun was high in the branches, and I lay in a shaft of light the colour of liquid honey. The treehouse smelled like bacon and coffee, but when I pulled back my bunk curtain, I found myself alone. On the folding table was a note:

> Off 2 community centre 4 hair washing — U should go 2.
> Mom et al

I made a BLT that spurted mayonnaise and tomato guts onto my pyjamas. Afterwards I brushed my teeth by the locker mirror above the porcelain wash bowl. Mom was definitely right about hair washing, I thought. Dreads were starting to form.

To make up for all the toffee I'd given Tilley, I'd gotten super-conscientious about my own teeth, and I brushed for the three full minutes recommended by the Dental Association. My mouth foamed with toothpaste, and I stepped onto the treehouse porch to spit. There was movement and a flash, and then, standing right in front of me was Kendra. My mouth fell open in surprise. Toothpaste foam cascaded down my chin. Kendra raised a camera.

"What are you doing?" I splattered. "Who invited you? Get out of here! You can't just barge into somebody's. . . ." I stopped.

"Into somebody's *what*?" Kendra asked. "Into somebody's *home*?"

I had no comeback. Standing there in my pyjamas, holding my toothbrush, I was pretty obviously at home. Kendra took a picture of my blank face.

"Stop doing that!" A glob of foam shot out in exclamation.

"Why? You don't look *that* much worse than usual." Kendra took another shot of my gross pyjamas and my street-person hair and my foaming mouth.

"Get! Out!" I advanced, brandishing my toothbrush.

"The true Rosie McGrady," Kendra said. "Captured at last in her own environment."

I had a sudden thought. "You followed me through the woods last night."

"Yeah, well, sorry to make you wet your pants and all," Kendra said. "I just had to see your fabulous *mansion* you've done all the bragging about. What a *surprise* to find nothing but some pathetic little treehouse."

"It's not pathetic."

"No? Let's see." Shoving past me, Kendra aimed her camera through the archway of the open treehouse door. I yanked her arm.

"I said *get out of here!*"

Kendra jerked her arm free. "Okay, don't spaz, I'm going. I've got what I need. Everybody at school is going to be *fascinated*."

"With my playhouse?" I said. But Kendra knew better.

"Oh *please*. Give it *up*, Rosie. Stop *lying*. We both know this is not your playhouse. It's your residential tree house—isn't that what you called it in your stupid contract with Eveline? This sad little place is where you *live*. You know it, and I know it, and pretty soon everybody at Windward is going to know it too. See you later."

Kendra started down the ladder, glancing up through the trap door to make sure I wasn't going to push her off. Pushing her off the ladder *was* an attractive idea, but I wasn't criminal enough to do it. I spat toothpaste over the banister and watched it wobble past her. She glared upward, and inexpertly descended the last rungs. I watched her head for the plank bridge.

Weak-kneed, I sat on the porch. I stared through the oak leaves that were just starting to uncurl. I'd done a ton of worrying over the past eight months, but what I felt at that moment was different. The feeling is hard to describe. I remember being electrocuted back in our old apartment when I stuck a knife inside the toaster. This feeling was sort of like that, but it kept on going. I guess the feeling was panic. I'd been caught. Kendra had photographs. Kendra had the contract with Eveline. Kendra had everything she needed, just like she said. Suddenly I was on my feet. I knew what I had to do. It was time to confess.

I knew it was important to get to Bridget first. To be worth anything, a confession has to be made before the secret gets out. Through the archway of the treehouse I saw my cell phone lying on our kitchen shelf. Not appropriate, I thought. Confessions have to be made in person. I had to get to Bridget's right away, before Kendra emailed the pictures. I scrambled down the ladder and yanked my bike from the shed. I rode like a fiend. The voltage of my electrocution increased the closer I got to Bridget's.

I stopped outside her house, flooded with doubt. I was in my tomato-guts pyjamas, and my hair was still unbrushed. Maybe I should have spent a few minutes fixing myself up? Looking repulsive was probably a big disadvantage during confession. But by then it was too late. I rang Bridget's bell. "Oh Rosie, hi," Paige said as she answered the door. Politely, she did not focus on my pyjamas. "Hang on, I'll get Bridget. BRIDGET!" Paige disappeared into the house, calling for her daughter.

When Paige came back Bridget was not with her. "Sorry, Rosie," Paige frowned. "It looks like Bridget's out." I thought Paige should know whether Bridget was out, but maybe that was just because I'd only ever lived in an apartment and a treehouse. Maybe in great big houses it was normal to not have a clue where anybody was.

"Can you ask her to call me?" I was sorry before I'd even finished asking. Now I'd just have to wait.

"Yes," Paige said. "I will."

"Okay. Thanks. Well, bye then."

Bridget did not call in the morning. I checked the battery of my cell and it was fine. I checked the ringer and it was on. It became afternoon, and I was still waiting for my phone to ring. I waited and waited, and the more I waited the more it did not ring. Sunday was the same. By dinnertime I couldn't stand it and I called her. There was no answer, which seemed weird for a Sunday night. I remembered that her family had call display.

By Monday morning I was a mess. I got to Windward early to look for Bridget. I didn't spot her, though, until everyone was filing inside after the nine o'clock bell. She was pretty far off and she didn't seem to see me. I jostled toward her. Bumping past other people, I arrived beside her. Her eyes stayed straight ahead and her jaw was set. I made myself look down at Bridget's wrist, and I found out what I needed to know. Where her friendship bracelet should have been, Bridget's wrist was bare. I walked backwards in front of her. "Bridget," I said. I was definitely in her field of vision, but she didn't focus. "Bridget," I said again, but she just stepped past me and through the classroom door. It was a very weird moment. It was as if there was some other person living in Bridget's body. It was like the real Bridget was gone, but it was also like I didn't exist either. It was as if where I stood there was nothing but the ghost of Bridget's friend.

I was paralyzed by these thoughts, so it was awhile before I noticed Kendra's pictures stuck on the bulletin board outside our classroom. Some were of the treehouse, but most were of me. Me in shrunken pyjamas, drooling toothpaste. Me, with greasy hair. Me, waving a toothbrush like a mental-case. Stupid, stupid, *stupid* me. I started taking them down.

"Go ahead, take them," Kendra said. "I'll print more. Or I'll just direct people to the website." I stuffed the pictures in my backpack.

When I walked into the classroom, everyone looked at me. Everyone except for Bridget, who stared straight ahead. Not once that morning did she look my way. At recess Bridget disappeared, and other people surrounded me.

"Is that *true*, that you live in a treehouse?" Sienna asked. I nodded.

"Bizarre!" said Nova.

"Aren't you just, like, totally *cramped*?" asked Twyla.

"Yeah, it's a bit cramped," I said.

"And you have no *electricity*?" Zach asked.

"Nope."

"I would hate that," Nova cried. "I would, like, completely die without Facebook."

"No plumbing either, Kendra says." This was from Matt.

"That is so gross!" said Twyla.

"I guess that explains her hair," said Sienna.

"And what, you just crap in the woods," asked Zach.

"Please," said Sienna. "I don't want to picture this."

"We have an outhouse," I said.

"Ew, I *despise* outhouses," said Sienna.

"The *smell*," said Twyla.

"The flies buzzing 'round your butt," said Heath.

"I'd kill myself," said Nova.

"What a weird family you have," Heath said, "to live in a treehouse."

"It's because they're on welfare," Sienna offered.

Devo approached. "Well, well," he said. "If it isn't Rosamund McGrady of *Bellemonde Drive*. Why all the BS about living in a mansion? Eh, McGrady? Why didn't you just admit that you live in some crappy little treehouse?"

"Didn't want to make you jealous," I replied.

"Jealous? Me?" said Devo.

"All of you," I said.

"Oh please," said Sienna.

"Like we'd be jealous of *you*," said Twyla.

"Thought you might be," I said. "But maybe not. Maybe you're all really happy locked up inside your great big houses. Operating your appliances. Breathing your special gourmet air. Guarded by your nannies. Whatever. To each his own." I brushed between Devo and Sienna.

As I walked away I thought about what had just happened. The people in my class had made fun of my home. It was exactly what I'd been afraid of. It was fear of exactly this that had made me turn my real life into a secret. I had invented a whole phony life to prevent exactly this. And now that it had actually happened, I found out that I didn't really care all that much. The scorn that I'd been so scared of was just not that big of a deal. This didn't make me feel any better though. It made me feel worse. It made me feel like I had lost my best friend completely, utterly, absolutely for nothing.

NOTEBOOK: #29

NAME: Rosamund McGrady

SUBJECT: The Present

I had some bad days after that.

I tried to talk to Bridget, but her reaction was always the same: no reaction. I couldn't keep putting myself through it. After a few tries I gave up.

Bridget started hanging out with Twyla, Sienna, Nova and Kendra again. It was some comfort that Bridget didn't seem to be having a lot of fun with them. It wasn't much though.

I held myself together at school. I didn't at home. I spent a lot of time in my middle bunk, face down, with my curtain pulled shut. "Rosie," Mom's voice would come through the curtain. "Rosie, what is it? What's wrong?"

"Nothing!" I'd shout into my foam mattress. I could just imagine the upbeat advice Mom would give me if I told her, and I was already mad at her for it.

Every day, Mom would ask about seventeen times what was wrong, and I always gave the same answer.

Nothing. One evening when Dad and Tilley had biked out to pick up pizza, Mom invaded my bunk. "Okay, you," she said. "I'm not leaving until you tell me about it." So finally I told. I told her everything. How I had pretended to live in Grand Oak Manor. How Kendra had found out the truth. How Bridget wasn't talking to me anymore.

"Oh, Rosie," Mom said, but she skipped the lecture that I expected about pretending to be something I wasn't. She just stroked the back of my hair. "Oh, sweetheart." I waited for her to say that this fight with Bridget would probably blow over. I intended to argue about it. Mom didn't say it though.

"It will probably blow over," I said, raising my head from the pillow.

"I hope so," Mom said, and I knew at that moment that it wouldn't.

---

Panther-Lamp Day arrived. Great-great-aunt Lydia seemed to be looking forward to it, so I continued with the sale at Grand Oak Manor, even though absolutely everybody knew by then that I didn't live there. The story about me living in a treehouse was all over Windward. Devo and Kendra and Co. bugged me about the treehouse, but hardly anybody else did. Most people at Windward were just interested, and a lot of them thought it sounded cool. I decided that I might as well add the treehouse to the Panther-Lamp-Day tour.

I spent the first part of Panther-Lamp Day at the treehouse. The turnout was huge. There was such a long lineup to go up the ladder that we had to declare a five-minute limit per visit. Each visit included a turn on the rope swing as the grand finale, but a lot of kids didn't have the nerve to do it and had to get back down to the ground by ladder. This slowed the tours and by the time I left the treehouse to go help Great-great-aunt Lydia, the lineup trailed across the meadow. I checked the lineup for Bridget. I hoped that maybe on my own territory, she might feel like she had to say something polite, and I could start a conversation. But Bridget was not there.

There were dozens and dozens of Windward people touring Grand Oak Manor, with Mr. Bickert as their miserable guide. I joined Great-great-aunt Lydia at the merchandise table in the dining room. Paige came in and bought a pair of candleholders. As Great-great-aunt Lydia counted out change, Paige chatted about how fabulous Grand Oak Manor was. She seemed kind of nervous. She didn't mention Bridget. When she finished praising the beautiful inglenook, whatever that is, she said she had to get going. "Goodbye, Rosie," she said. She stopped and then gave me a big hug, which is something she'd never done before. I didn't trust myself to open my mouth. I just turned and waggled my fingers over my shoulder.

Bridget's birthday was at the end of May. Her party was laser tag. I know, because I saw Kendra's invitation on her desk. The party was Saturday, May 29, from six to nine-thirty. On the night of the party Mom said it was too warm and beautiful to be indoors playing laser tag. "Yeah," I said. It seemed like a lot of trouble to say. I couldn't do anything that night between six and nine-thirty except lie on the porch, staring past the leaves into space. I watched Venus appear in the sky, and then Jupiter, and then Mars.

At nine-thirty, when the far-away party guests were thanking Bridget and Paige, and getting into their SUVs, I picked myself off the porch. I climbed into bed, curled against the hours ahead.

That was a low point. It isn't all as bad as that. There has been some good stuff too.

Tilley and I made up, for one thing.

"I don't like Eveline," Tilley announced a couple of days after Kendra invaded the treehouse.

"Good call," I said, surprised. "Why not?"

"Cause Eveline told about the tree house! She told Kendra!"

"Why did she?"

"Cause Kendra paid her! I said that was against the contract. Eveline said too bad, cause Kendra paid her lots. I said that wasn't fair, cause you did all the things we specified. Eveline said I was stupid. I said she was mean. I said she wasn't my friend anymore."

As soon as Eveline's evil influence ended, Tilley turned nice again. One Saturday I got home from washing my hair at the community centre to see all of my stuff moved back up to the top bunk. The yellow-crested something had come back and laid three eggs, and I thought it was nice of Tilley to give up her bedside view of the nest. The eggs have hatched since then. Tilley comes up to the top berth a lot, and we sit and watch the scrawny baby birds being fed.

As soon as Tilley and I were friends again, I told her and Mom and Dad everything I had found out about Tavish and Great-great-aunt Lydia and Mr. Bickert. They were all excited, even Dad, and we all went for afternoon tea at

Grand Oak Manor. The tea was a success. Great-great-aunt Lydia offered to learn the language that Mom is developing for ape-human communication, and now Mom is teaching her. It is weird beyond words to witness Mom and Great-great-aunt Lydia greeting each other in this language, but weird in a good way.

I go for tea at Grand Oak Manor a lot. The teas have improved. Great-great-aunt Lydia still has her beige biscuits, but now her three-storey platter is loaded up with these fancy little cakes like what Marie Antoinette would eat. She must be forcing Mr. Bickert to go out and buy them. So far none of the cakes have been poisoned. With all the teas, I'm getting to know Great-great-aunt Lydia pretty well. It doesn't even bother me anymore when she falls asleep mid-sentence.

So that's it. That's the present.

Things change. People adjust.

I guess I still miss Bridget though. I guess that's the feeling that's still at the back of my throat.

## *August 27*

*I would love to read what Rosamund wrote.*

*But I'm not to call her that.*

*"Great-great-aunt Lydia," she asked me one teatime. "Do you think you could start calling me Rosie?"*

*"You don't like Rosamund?" I asked her.*

*"Not really. It's sort of an old lady name." She touched her mouth. "No offence."*

*"No, you have a point," I said. "I feel the same about being called Great-great-aunt Lydia. It's rather forbidding, don't you think?"*

*So we agreed. I'm to call her Rosie and she's to call me Auntie Liddie, which I know perfectly well does not suit me in the least. It's cheerier than I have ever managed to be, but I like it, so Auntie Liddie it is. Rosie remembers most of the time.*

*She wrote for weeks. Through my binoculars I watched her cross-legged on the treehouse porch, her pen suspended in thought. I watched her sprawled on the meadow, filling page after page, crawling every now and then to follow the shade of the cherry tree. And all those rainy days, I watched her here, in the turret, tucked up in the armchair just across from me. Outside was a waterfall of summer rain, and inside was a rare peace, punctuated only by Mr. Bickert bringing fresh pots of tea.*

*"You're quite the writer," I said one of those summer days. She'd reached the end of a notebook and her face parted the*

*curtain of her copper hair. "Is it a novel you're working on?"*

*"No," she said. She put the notebook in her backpack and took a fresh one out. "It's my true story. About the treehouse."*

*"Ah. And an interesting story it is." I let her get back to her writing.*

*Then days went by when Rosie did not have her pen and notebook. "Have you stopped working on your true story," I asked one teatime.*

*"I finished."*

*I said what I'd been wondering. "Am I allowed to read them? Your notebooks?"*

*Rosie looked at me. "I don't have them anymore."*

*"Not have them! Why? Why not? What's happened to them?"*

*"I gave them to Bridget. Sort of. I left them outside her front door. In a cardboard box. With a note."*

*"Your true story was all for Bridget?"*

*"Yeah, it was. Because I told her all those fake stories. And she doesn't understand why. I was trying to explain."*

*"That's a long explanation."*

*"I know. I never thought it would get that long. Like, I definitely did not expect to write 29 whole notebooks. But once I got started, I just felt like telling her everything. You know? Because she really wanted to know me. When we were friends, she wanted to know everything about me, and how often does that happen? And I blew it. I totally blew it. I wanted to be my real self with her, at least once, and the notebooks were my last chance."*

*"You're right that it's a rare thing," I said finally. "For someone to want to really know you."*

*"But she doesn't anymore. Now she's just mad at me. I don't know if she'll even read the notebooks. She'll probably just dump them in the recycling."*

*"Tell me that you at least kept a copy."*

*"Like a photocopy? No. I didn't. It would have been really expensive."*

*I took a moment. "I would have paid for the photocopying," I said. I would have paid a lot, for a story in which I had a role.*

*"Oh. Well. I didn't know," Rosie said. "I guess it's too late now." Both of us gazed into the vacant space of the turret until Mr. Bickert entered with a tray of the petits fours that Rosie likes so much.*

*The weeks went by. Neither of us mentioned the absent notebooks again. The summer rains stopped, the clouds went their separate ways, and the sky became a continual blue. And then came that August afternoon.*

*I keep seeing what Rosie described. I can see her wading through the tall blonde meadow grass in the shimmering heat. I can see her picking daisies and bachelor buttons, using two hands to tear the tough stems. I can see her sorting her flowers as she enters the green shade of the giant oak. She looks up and sees Bridget.*

*Rosie opens her mouth and closes it. Bridget says, "I read your notebooks."*

*"Oh."*

*"Yeah. I read them. And. I came to see the baby birds. The yellow-crested somethings?"*

*"Oh, yeah. Them. They're gone."*

*"They flew the nest?"*

*"A long time ago."*

*"Oh," Bridget shrugs. "They sounded cute."*

*"Do you want a tour?" Rosie says. "While you're here?"*

*"Okay."*

*"It's this way." Rosie points up the tree trunk. "I guess you know that."*

*Rosie climbs the ladder and Bridget follows. They go through the trap door and the arched doorway. "The bunks," Rosie points. "The bunk curtains. The propane fridge."*

*"It's just like in the notebooks."*

*"The cast-iron stove. The camping stove." Rosie is expressionless, but she can't help it. The same thing seems to be wrong with Bridget.*

*"Hunh," Bridget says.*

*They go out on the porch. "The water pump." Rosie says. "The porch. I guess that's obvious. The trap door. But you saw that on your way up. So. I guess that's about it."*

*"Hunh," Bridget says, and for a moment there is just the soft hum of insects. "Well, I guess I should get—"*

*"I forgot the rope swing."*

*"Right."*

*Rosie leads Bridget up the ladder that rises from the trap door. On the platform she hoists up the wooden seat. "Like this." Rosie jumps. She falls and falls, then the rope tightens, and she sails toward the sky with every emotion ripped free and left behind. When the swing slows, Rosie climbs back to Bridget.*

*"I guess it's my turn," Bridget says. She straddles the seat and looks down and the minutes go by. Then she jumps and screams and the rope snaps tight and her breath is snatched away. When Rosie gets to the bottom of the ladder Bridget is still arcing back and forth. Finally she jumps to the ground. She looks as though she might cry. "Omigosh! That was SO much fun!" Bridget is grinning ear to ear and instantly Rosie is too. It's broken, that curse of being unable to produce a smile.*

*Rosie notices something. "Bridget! You got braces!"*

*"Two days ago. I hate them! They've got built-in screws to increase the pressure. Like medieval instruments of torture." Bridget opens wide, and Rosie peers inside her mouth.*

*"They look cruel," Rosie says.*

*"They probably violate some international convention."*

*"Want to swing again?"*

*"Yeah," says Bridget. "It distracts me from my suffering."*

*Bridget stays for the afternoon. She and Rosie swing and swing, and when they get too hot they swish themselves around in the stream. Drying off in the meadow, they describe what they see in the cumulus clouds. Bridget sees a yak; Rosie sees the devil in a tutu. At dinnertime Bridget calls home on her cell phone and gets permission to stay. They cook dinner by campfire and they blister their marshmallows over the embers. Bridget is escorted home in darkness, guided by headlamps.*

*I've often reflected on that summer day. Rosie's day. It's as vivid to me as if it were my own memory, although memory is a funny thing at my age. Things I'm told I did yesterday leave not a trace in my mind.*

*Clearer than my own memories are my dreams. Yesterday's visit from Tavish is so clear. His laugh and his hand on my arm. It's hard to believe that none of it was real, even though the obituary on my desk proves that he's been dead nine years.*

*And clearer than my own memories are Rosie's. I'm discovering the pleasure of adopting another's memory as one's own. That's what I've done with Rosie and Bridget's reunion. I've likely supplied a detail or two of my own, but the scene that plays itself in my mind is essentially what Rosie told me. It's not one of my armchair dreams, I'm quite sure of that. After all, I often see the two of them from the turret, with my binoculars, as they flash out on the rope swing: the sweep of Bridget's dark hair, alternating with Rosie's strawberry blonde.*

*I might get to read Rosie's notebooks now. I am going to ask her, the next time that she comes for tea. She doesn't come for tea quite so often anymore, but I suppose that is as it should be. Sunny young girls are not meant to spend too much time shut indoors with gloomy old ladies. And I'm glad that Rosie and Bridget have managed to repair their friendship. Some things are more valuable, it seems, for having been damaged and repaired. I'm glad when my binocular lens finds the girls laughing. I am. I'm glad to watch them having fun. I welcome the thought of them swinging together over our meadow, for the rest of my days, and beyond.*

# Acknowledgements

My thanks to those who took a chance on this book. I'm honoured by your faith. In particular, thank you to my agent Carolyn Swayze, for letting me catch her much-sought attention, and to my editor Linda Pruessen for her easygoing but great advice. And thanks also to my husband, for support expressed in so many ways.